SPY CAT
BLACKOUT

ANDREW COPE

Illustrated by James de la Rue

PUFFIN

PUFFIN BOOKS

Published by the Penguin Group
Penguin Books Ltd, 80 Strand, London WC2R 0RL, England
Penguin Group (USA) Inc., 375 Hudson Street, New York, New York 10014, USA
Penguin Group (Canada), 90 Eglinton Avenue East, Suite 700, Toronto, Ontario, Canada M4P 2Y3
(a division of Pearson Penguin Canada Inc.)
Penguin Ireland, 25 St Stephen's Green, Dublin 2, Ireland (a division of Penguin Books Ltd)
Penguin Group (Australia), 707 Collins Street, Melbourne, Victoria 3008, Australia
(a division of Pearson Australia Group Pty Ltd)
Penguin Books India Pvt Ltd, 11 Community Centre, Panchsheel Park, New Delhi – 110 017, India
Penguin Group (NZ), 67 Apollo Drive, Rosedale, Auckland 0632, New Zealand
(a division of Pearson New Zealand Ltd)
Penguin Books (South Africa) (Pty) Ltd, Block D, Rosebank Office Park,
181 Jan Smuts Avenue, Parktown North, Gauteng 2193, South Africa

Penguin Books Ltd, Registered Offices: 80 Strand, London WC2R 0RL, England

puffinbooks.com

First published 2014
001

Set in 15/18 pt Bembo Book MT Std
Typeset by Jouve (UK), Milton Keynes
Printed in Great Britain by Clays Ltd, St Ives plc

British Library Cataloguing in Publication Data
A CIP catalogue record for this book is available from the British Library

ISBN: 978-0-141-34722-6

www.greenpenguin.co.uk

Penguin Books is committed to a sustainable
future for our business, our readers and our planet.
This book is made from Forest Stewardship
Council™ certified paper.

Sometimes ideas fly into my head in the middle of the day. Sometimes when I'm in the bath or when I'm at Tesco's. I even have a pencil and paper at my bedside in case anything comes to me in a dream. But sometimes it's a whole lot easier to just borrow ideas off people who are much better at writing than me! People like Will Hussey. Thanks for inspiring me, matey.

Contents

Contents

1. A Crooked Lady

It was a sticky night. The moon's reflection shimmered on the Mediterranean Sea. The cruise ship anchored offshore twinkled like a thousand stars. The passengers had retired to their cabins, exhausted after a day of sight-seeing. The food and wine had been top-notch on this, the most exclusive of luxury cruises. Despite the heat, there was no tossing and turning. All the passengers had attended the captain's supper and were fast asleep, drugged by the thief that was now systematically raiding their cabins.

It was frustrating being in a wheelchair. This was the biggest and best cruise ship, with miles of corridors and too many tight corners. But the thief consoled herself that she had all night. The electric wheelchair hissed down the

executive-suite corridor. It turned sharp left. Stopped. Reversed. Sharp left again. A couple of centimetres forward and it was pointing straight at cabin number one.

The thief rummaged in her handbag. 'Now where are my glasses?' she murmured, her fingers grasping at an assortment of pills and boiled sweets. 'Deary me.' She was about to give up and return to her own cabin to find her spectacles when she remembered. Her bony fingers went to her white hair and she chuckled. 'On my head, where they always are. Oh, Iris, you'd forget your own head if it wasn't screwed on.'

The old lady wrestled her glasses out of a tangle of hair and fixed them on to her face. She peered at the cabin number and a veiny hand ran down her list. 'Cabin one . . . Lord and Lady Hesketh-Brown. Perfect.'

She opened her purse and rummaged again. This was the slowest robbery in history and, confined to a wheelchair, it was also destined to be the slowest getaway. *But*, she considered, *that's the point, isn't it? Too many people are rushing around. The modern world is too quick*. Her mission was to slow it down. And the plot was to start right here, with the Hesketh-Browns. She pulled out some old bus tickets. 'Nope.' Mint Imperials. 'Nope.' Her faltering eyes picked out the credit-card room key. Iris tutted. *What's wrong with old-fashioned keys?* she thought. *Heavy ones that you put into a lock and twisted?* She leant forward and slipped the credit card into the slot. A green light came on and she tutted again. *Flashing lights in doors? Whatever next?*

She pushed the handle forward and her wheelchair bumped the door open. The criminal pensioner whirred almost silently into the room. The Hesketh-Browns were out cold so noise didn't matter. Lord Hesketh was in his

silk pyjamas, mouth open, dribbling slightly. Lady Hesketh retained a little dignity, head lolled to one side, a book fallen in her lap. The TV was on. 'Ooh,' smiled the old lady, '*Gone with the Wind*, one of my favourites.'

But she knew she didn't have time to watch TV. Her mission was clear. The wheelchair bumped and banged its way past the bed, towards the safe. The thief knew she'd never remember the code so had written it down in a little black book. She peered down through her spectacles and then hit the keypad. She entered the first number and the keypad beeped. Then there was an age as she looked down at her paper, her shaking hand searching for the second number.

Five beeps later her bony finger had tapped out the sequence and the slowest robbery in history had truly begun. Another green light and the safe door swung open. The thief's beady eyes shone as brightly as the diamonds within. 'Bingo!' she grinned.

Her hand reached in and scooped out the diamonds. She cupped them in her right palm, thinking how pleased her boss would be. The old lady opened her purse and poured them in before clicking it closed and swinging the safe shut. The wheelchair reversed, the driver too old to bend her neck and look where she was going. 'Oh bother!' She hit a table and a vase crashed to the floor. His Lord and Her Ladyship snored on, unaware that their treasure was disappearing at pensioner speed.

The wheelchair whirred in reverse, hitting the desk and bed. Eventually it hissed backwards, into the executive-suite corridor, and the cabin door clicked shut. The diamond thief's grin was so big that her false teeth nearly fell out. She fixed her lower set back in place and consulted her list.

Iris was proud to be living out every definition of the word 'crooked'. *Cabin sixteen next*, she thought, easing her motorized wheelchair forward. *The Brockman-Smythes. They're worth a small fortune.*

2. Hosepipe Ban

Shakespeare was proud to be part of the family. He fitted in well and was thoroughly enjoying his two roles. He was playing the 'traditional cat' role, which involved sitting on people's knees, sleeping on duvets, snaking round ankles and treating the family home like a hotel. He was also doing what he called 'cat chores' and was especially proud of how he'd rid the house of mice. He doubted the Cook family even knew they had a mouse infestation. But he'd worked tirelessly, mostly after dark, using his night-vision to seek them out and his sharp claws to scare them away. He'd decided not to kill the mice. *I'll just put the frighteners on them*, he thought.

He was adored by the kids, particularly Sophie. And he was especially delighted with

the way he'd managed to get along with the dogs. In feline folklore, cats failed to mix with two things: water and dogs. Kittens were taught from an early age that both were evil. Water was OK – if you were desperate that is – as a drink. But it came way down the pecking order: miles below cream (number 1), milk (2) and tea (3). Yet cats' failure to swim was legendary so open water was to be avoided. As were dogs. The canine v. feline wars had raged since the battle of 1632. Cats were taught that dogs started it. Canines vice versa. The facts had been forgotten years ago. Either way, there was a general hatred between the species. But Shakespeare had learnt that cats and dogs can be best buddies. All you needed was an open mind and a positive attitude.

Shakespeare marvelled at the family's head dog. The Cook family had adopted Lara, code-named GM451, from the RSPCA. Although little did they know that in reality it had been Lara who had adopted them. Lara stood for Licenced Assault and Rescue Animal, and she was the world's first ever Spy Dog, a highly trained secret agent who was now posing as an ordinary family pet. But Shakespeare had learnt there was nothing 'ordinary' about Lara. Any dog who could ride a bike, play the guitar and surf the Internet was a pretty cool mutt. And now Shakespeare had the opportunity to be part of the team, learning the ropes and becoming the world's first ever Spy Cat.

Professor Cortex was the mastermind behind Lara's accelerated learning programme. And now Shakespeare was catching up fast. The scientist didn't call him Shakespeare. To the professor, Shakespeare was 'Agent CAT' or 'Classified Animal Trainee'.

Except I don't want to be a trainee any more, thought Shakespeare. *I want to be a proper qualified spy. Solving crimes, fighting evil, sweeping the streets clean of baddies. If GM451 is the coolest dog on the planet, I want to be the coolest puss.*

Shakespeare had already had one adventure. *A sort of practice mission*, he thought. His paw went to a ripped ear, a souvenir of a close encounter with an evil baddie. He glanced in the mirror, reassuring himself that his translating pet collar was still flashing. *This collar is the professor's finest invention*, he thought. *It allows me to understand human language and read human writing.*

Although Shakespeare had conquered his fear of dogs, he had a very special reason to be terrified of water. Sitting on one of the highest branches in the beech tree, he shuddered at the sight of the squirting hosepipe below. Ben, Sophie and Ollie loved the sunshine and had taken advantage by getting into their swimming costumes and splashing around in a small inflatable paddling pool. Ben had arranged the slide so they could plunge into the cold water. There was plenty of joyful screaming and excited splashing. Shakespeare watched, unblinking, from the shade of the tree. Inside he was shrieking with horror. *Water and cats don't mix!*

His cat's eyes peered from the tree as he watched the puppies joining in. Star was first down the slide, hitting the water with a howl of glee. Spud was next. He stood at the top of the slide, blowing kisses to the audience, before launching his furry tummy down the slide and hitting the water with an enormous puppy splash.

'Nice one, Spud,' yelled Sophie. 'A doggy bellyflop!' Water sloshed over the side and Ollie took charge of the hosepipe, squirting more ice-cold water into the pool.

Shakespeare's tail swished. *There's only one thing worse than water and that's cold water!*

Spud splashed his way out of the pool and stood, shaking from nose to tail, water spraying everywhere. He eyed Shakespeare sitting in the tree. 'Come on down, puss,' he woofed. 'The water's lovely.'

Shakespeare dug his claws into the branch and shuddered again, terrible memories flooding his head. He watched a little longer, wincing uneasily. *I need to take my mind off it*, he thought, grabbing his iPad and climbing even higher, making sure he was out of range of the snaking hosepipe.

The cat lodged his iPad against a branch and clicked on to the Internet. His collar blinked brightly as he settled on to the BBC news page. *The usual stuff*, he noted. *Boring business reports, celebrity tittle-tattle and rain on the way*. He stifled a yawn and stretched, considering a catnap. *But here's an interesting one*, he thought, clicking on to a news item about an Internet blackout in Wales.

He watched a short Internet news clip, delivered by a worried Welsh reporter who'd driven over the border into England to deliver the message. 'I'm unable to send you this report from Wales,' she said, creases etched into her brow. 'Satellite communications are down and all Internet and mobile-phone connections have been lost. The country has ground to a halt. Wales is, quite literally, offline.'

Shakespeare loved the Internet. It was the source of all his information and he enjoyed playing Xbox Live with Spud and Star. His paw went to his translating collar. *I'm not sure how this works*, he thought. *But I suspect there's a*

Wi-Fi connection involved somewhere. He glanced down at the fun below. *Yes, water is bad. But going offline is probably worse*.

His name was Eddie, but his team knew him only as 'the Past Master'. At eighty, he was the youngest in the room. The old man's arthritic hands fumbled with the parcel. He reached for a knife and slid it down the side of the brown paper, easing the box out of its wrapping. A postcard fell out and he smiled at the swirly writing.

He looked around at his assembled team. 'It's from Iris,' he announced. 'From the cruise ship. It's got a stamp on, from Italy.'

'Oooh,' gasped the audience, sitting up in their chairs.

'What does it say?' inquired one of the pensioners, fiddling with his hearing aid.

For a moment, the Past Master was lost in thoughts of the holidays he used to have. *Seaside trips, donkey rides, bucket and spade, rolled-up trouser legs*. He fought back a tear. *Good times*. *And such innocent fun*. He considered it a shame that hardly anyone sent postcards any more. *It was one of life's little pleasures: going to the seaside, choosing your postcards and scribbling the headline news of your holiday adventures*. *And*, he remembered, *sometimes the postal service was so slow that you'd beat your postcard home*.

He thought about his own children, all grown up, and seven great-grandchildren. *None of them have ever sent me a postcard*, he thought.

Sometimes they show me their pictures, on a tiny screen on their new-fangled mobile phones. But with my eyesight . . .

The Past Master composed himself. He perched his reading glasses on the end of his nose and scanned Iris's writing, her style all loopy and swirly. *And that's another thing*, he considered. *Handwriting isn't what it used to be. It's all text language and slang. 'LOL' indeed!* Eddie didn't have a mobile phone. He sometimes sat and listened to his great-grandchildren and struggled to comprehend what they were talking about. He longed for the day when 'pants' meant undergarments, 'sick' was vomit and 'wicked' described an evil witch.

He cleared his throat before reading the postcard aloud. 'Having a fabulous time and I have been productive,' he began, beaming at his audience. 'I've met lots of lovely people. Easy pickings. Please find enclosed eighteen of what you wanted. Wish you were here. Yours sincerely, Iris.'

'Oooh, she's having a good time then,' nodded one of the old ladies in the team. 'I hope she's not had any tummy troubles. That foreign water always disagrees with me.'

'I was in Italy,' piped up a voice from the back. 'During the war.'

Silence fell once more as the Past Master opened the small box. He tipped it up and eighteen diamonds cascaded on to the table.

His eyes sparkled. 'We're nearly there, everybody. Just a few more robberies and we'll have enough diamonds to take the whole of Europe offline.'

3. Daylight Robbery

This time it was daylight robbery. The Orient Express prided itself on the fact that it was the world's most expensive train ride. London to Venice, in total luxury. The manager was delighted to have a full train and, as always, the price meant no riff-raff. The cabins were small put perfectly equipped. The food was cooked by the finest chefs and served by the world's stiffest waiters and waitresses.

The train had hardly pulled out of London before the passengers had been approached. 'Champagne, madam?' offered the waiter, hoping his grin would eventually earn him a massive tip.

'Not for me, deary,' nodded the elderly lady, sitting alone, reading a romance novel. 'Gives me, you know . . . wind,' she said, mouthing the final word of the sentence and waving her hand at her nose.

'Quite, madam,' agreed the waiter, his smile sagging ever so slightly.

'And so does posh food. But I like pork chops. And Spam. I do hope you can serve me some Spam. I've still got my own teeth.' She grinned scarily to reveal a row of mostly gaps. 'It's twelve o'clock you know,' she said, tapping her watch impatiently. 'I always have my lunch at twelve. On the dot. And I'd love some sherry. I'll tell you what,' she suggested 'why don't you have my champagne and I'll have a drop of sherry. In fact,' beamed the old lady, her wrinkles gouging even deeper, 'I insist.'

The waiter, sniffing a lonely old lady whom he could befriend and get written into the will of, jumped at the chance. He served the other passengers in double-quick time before bringing the old lady a very large sherry and parking himself opposite her. This time his grin was genuine. It wasn't often he got to sip the expensive stuff.

'I'm Margaret,' said the old lady, offering a hand that was mostly knuckles. 'Do you know how old I am, young man?'

The waiter took Margaret's fingers and shook

her hand. 'I've no idea! Twenty-one perhaps?' he said cheesily, thinking 121 was closer to the truth.

The old lady cackled. 'I can't remember,' she said. 'I stopped counting after ninety.'

He lifted his champagne and the lady raised her sherry. 'To the journey of a lifetime, Marge,' he proposed.

'Believe you me, young man,' smiled Margaret, her remaining teeth glowing yellow, 'it will be.'

Shakespeare had forgotten about his catnap. He was totally engrossed in the news. While the children and dogs splashed below, he clicked on several news channels. *They're all saying the same thing. Wales is having an Internet blackout. It seems there's no TV, Wi-Fi, Internet, satnav, email or mobile-phone signals. How weird.*

He checked Twitter. A picture taken by an amateur astronomer showed an explosion in space. *Welsh comms satellite goes bang #nightmare #walesdown* read the caption.

He clicked on another message: *Wales satellite shot down #interNOT*.

Shakespeare's spine tingled with excitement. *Someone's shooting satellites to smithereens*. How he longed for an adventure like this.

The Orient Express powered through the Channel Tunnel. Margaret was hugely disappointed that it was such a modern train. She'd been hoping for a steam train. *Like in the olden days*. She longed for those times when engines chugged through the countryside, smoke billowing, whistle tooting, with the driver's mate shovelling coal into the furnace. The 'Orient Express' had sounded so romantic. *Old-fashioned even. And here we are, whizzing underneath the sea at 120 mph*. Margaret was in no rush. 'Romance is well and truly dead,' she tutted as she struggled to raise herself from her seat.

Everyone else was sleeping, intoxicated by too much of Margaret's drugged champagne. She tottered to her feet and picked up her walking stick. She swayed down the aisle, a little tipsy after a midday sherry and her hip playing up. She plonked herself down with the first group of sleeping passengers.

'Hellooo!' yelled the pensioner. 'Mr Baxter, can you hear me?' The family snored on. Margaret took her walking stick and prodded the man in his chest. Still nothing. It was fiddly trying to undo Mrs Baxter's necklace so the old lady reached into her handbag for her nail scissors. She snipped the thread and the diamonds poured off. One or two fell to the floor, but Margaret caught what she could and spread them out on the table.

'Oh, the Past Master will be pleased,' she purred. She unscrewed the bottom of her walking stick, turned the stick upside down and, one by one, dropped the diamonds inside. It took an age but she didn't mind. After screwing the end back on, she checked Mr Baxter for valuables, just in case. He had 3,000 euros of spending money in his wallet, a £5,000 watch, a 24-carat gold wedding ring and emerald cufflinks. The old lady tutted. 'No diamonds – useless.'

She leant on her stick and raised herself to her feet. She tottered to the next group of dozing passengers and her search for diamonds continued.

4. Posh Nosh

The day was over. Shakespeare had avoided the paddling pool and had absorbed every piece of news he could. His overworked iPad was recharging, as was he, curled up at the foot of Sophie's bed. His body twitched and his eyelids flickered as a nightmare ripped through his sleep.

It had started as a strange slow-motion dream. He was floating in space, a fishbowl on his head, trying to grab pieces of satellite as they floated past. 'The world is depending on you, space puss,' said Ollie's voice. Then, to Shakespeare's horror, the fishbowl started filling up. The water was up to his mouth, then his nose. Shakespeare twitched in his sleep. 'I can't breathe,' he gurgled as a goldfish swam past his eyes . . .

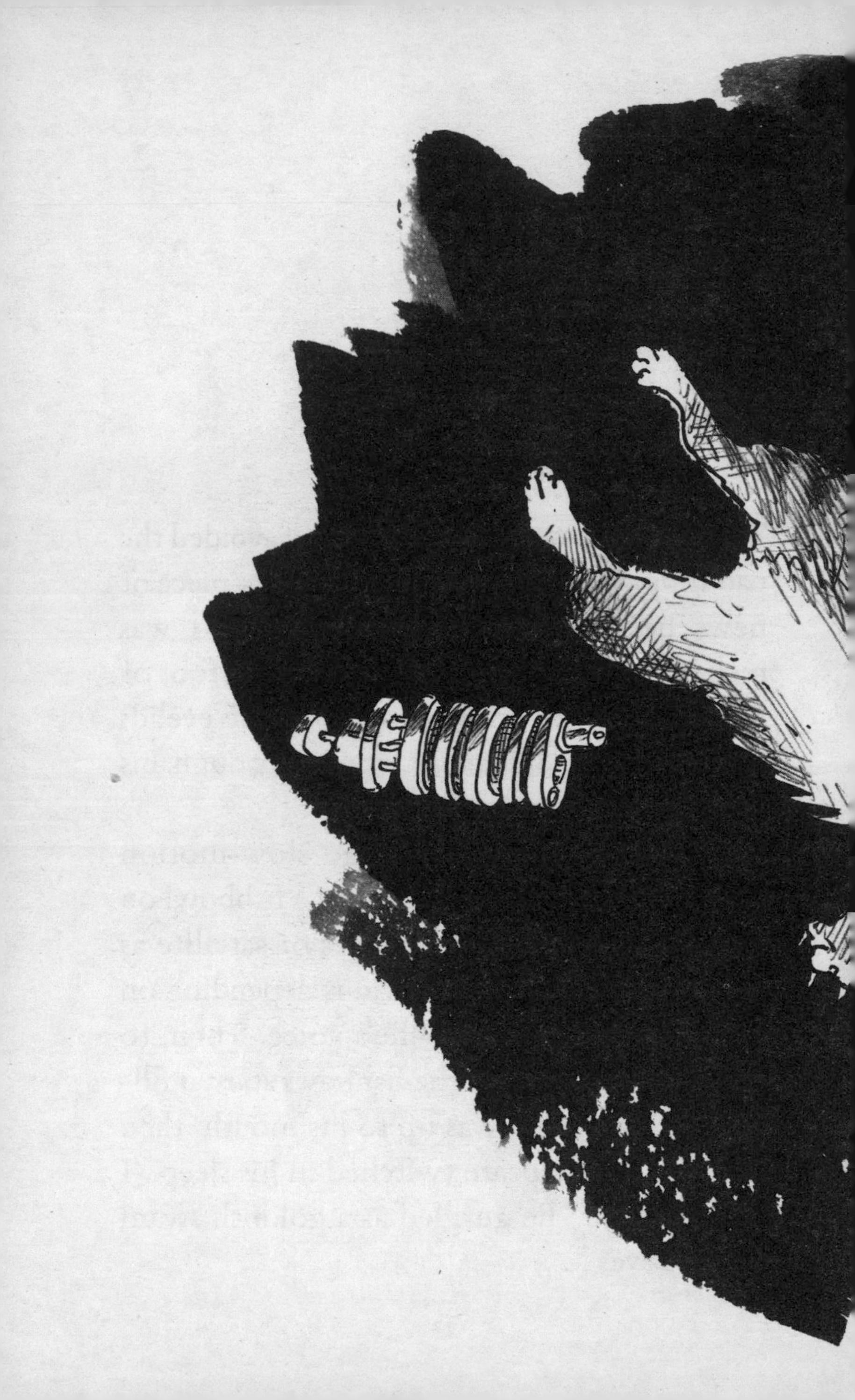

The next moment his nightmare brought him back to earth with a bang. There was no spacesuit, just a huge man leering at him. 'No, please. Not me,' he meowed as the man bent down and caught him by the scruff of his tiny kitten neck. Shakespeare's body kicked in his sleep as the man scooped him into the sack, where he wriggled for freedom with his brothers and sisters. Then it all went dark, and hot, as the sack was tied and slung over the man's shoulder. The eight kittens kept still, trying to stay comfortable as the man marched across the fields. Then he stopped.

Shakespeare could smell water. His nose twitched. *Flowing water. Probably a river?* And there was a terrible moment when the sack was thrown through the air before splashing in. It took a few seconds before water started seeping into the sack. There was panic among his brothers and sisters as they struggled in the darkness. Shakespeare could feel the sack being dragged by the current. *We're flowing with the river and sinking*, he thought as the water got higher. He had no choice but to stand on his brother's head to claw at the top of the sack. Shakespeare could hear his siblings meowing for their lives. It was hot. And dark. *And getting wetter by the second.* He clawed again and daylight broke through. The sack was half full by now, and he reached down and pulled his baby sister out of the water at the bottom of the bag. He lifted her to safety. She was mewing very quietly. *Probably in shock.*

'Don't give up,' meowed Shakespeare, leaping at the top of the sack and creating a hole large enough to scrabble through. He hauled himself out and lowered his paw. One by one, his brothers and sisters were heaved out and they leapt for their lives, plunging into the river, paddling frantically. 'Swim for it,' he meowed, his eyes scanning for the best way to ensure his own survival.

Seven cats were struggling through the water towards the bank on his right, but the sack had drifted and he calculated that the left bank might be a better bet. His mind was working overtime. *It's less steep so, if I make it, I'll have a chance of clambering on to dry land.* Shakespeare had no time to think any more. Kittens' ears were bobbing about to his right. *They can't swim! I just hope they learn fast!*

If I stay put, I'll drown. His brothers and sisters were paddling for their lives, ears and noses just about staying above water. *If I go right, I'll drown. If I swim left, I might drown.* All the options were bad.

The sack had finally sunk and, the decision made for him, his legs were kicking and he could feel the cold water chilling his tiny body. *I hate water*! Shakespeare's back legs kicked out for the left-hand bank . . .

. . . and the huge effort woke him with a jolt. The cat gasped for breath and he came to his

senses. His fur was standing on end. His heart was pounding and his breathing quick.

Water! It's no wonder it's my worst nightmare.

He'd survived being thrown into a river, but he wondered if his brothers and sisters had made it.

Gordon Blooming-Whittingstall was bellowing at his staff. 'It's celebrity night at Numero Uno,' he yelled. 'And we've got a restaurant full of top-notch A-listers. These people are dripping with fame and wealth. They are used to the best. They expect the best. And tonight, you muppets, we will give them the best meal they've ever had.'

The head chef's hat was sagging under the strain. Gordon Blooming-Whittingstall spent all his time cooking on TV and had actually forgotten how to cook in real life. If his wife wanted him to make beans on toast, she had to follow him around with a camcorder while he explained how to heat the beans. But that didn't stop him shouting. He noticed the pile of washing-up was getting bigger. 'You're daydreaming again, Reg!' he bellowed to the oldest person in the kitchen, a man of about forty who was up to his elbows in soapsuds.

'Sorry, boss,' said the man, plunging his hands back into the dirty water.

Washing pots was the lowest level of the food chain. The washer-upper had nobody to shout at. Most kitchens used young people as pot-washers. But Gordon Blooming-Whittingstall had driven all the youngsters away. The only person who he could get to stick at the job was Reg. Reg had lasted almost a week, reliably (and very slowly) washing the dishes.

Reg didn't mind. The Past Master had sent him on a mission and he didn't care how he was being treated because tonight was going to be his night. He loved washing up, especially the old-fashioned way with rubber gloves and suds. But it was hot in the kitchen and his disguise was melting. His wig was itchy and his make-up had begun to run down his neck. He was thankful that all the staff were too busy to look very closely. If they had, they'd have noticed signs of his real age. The big ears, extra-long nose hairs and the fact that his trousers were pulled up almost to his nipples.

He was glad of the bright yellow gloves. Not only did they protect his hands from the boiling water, they also hid his eighty-four-year-old fingers. His bony knuckles were almost impossible to disguise so the best thing was to keep them hidden. Nobody would employ an eighty-four-year-old so he was doing his best to act like a man half his age. He stood as tall as his bent spine would allow.

Reg studied the craziness of the kitchen. A small colony of workers scurrying around like ants under a rock.

The old man looked at the plates of food that were 'ready to go' to table 16. *Why is modern food always arranged in towers?* he thought. *And why no gravy? And why do they have such huge plates with hardly any food on them? And what on earth is 'couscous'?* He thought back to his day. *A large plate of piping-hot meat and two veg, swimming in gravy. Always with potatoes. No fancy pasta or rice. And certainly no couscous. We had proper food*, he thought, *and it never did us any harm*. Reg was motivated by the thought that it wouldn't be long before those days returned.

'I said stop daydreaming, Reg!' bellowed the restaurant owner. 'There's no slacking in my kitchen. We need two hundred clean glasses because I'm about to do a toast to our wonderful customers to thank them for attending our celebrity night.'

Reg smiled a wry smile. His moment had almost arrived. He'd seen to it personally that each bottle of bubbly had been injected with a sleeping potion. Trays of the stuff were being sent into the restaurant. Reg slipped off his yellow gloves and listened while Gordon proposed a toast and all the customers raised their glasses. 'To Numero Uno,' sang Gordon.

There was a loud chant of 'Numero Uno!', lots of clinking of glasses and then Gordon reeled off a terribly cheesy speech. There was a round of applause and then all the celebrities rekindled their conversations, bragging about their latest reality TV projects.

Reg took charge of the kitchen staff. 'Ladies and gents,' he beamed. 'We have pulled it off. We've served two hundred minor celebrities the most overpriced meal they've ever had. And Gordon's never going to thank us. So I propose we have a sip of his best champagne and toast ourselves.'

The worker ants cheered. 'Great idea, Reg,' grinned the chef, sweat dripping into the saucepan he was stirring.

Reg led by example. He raised a glass of fizzy water, his ancient hand shaking just a little. 'To us,' he pronounced. 'The best kitchen team in the world, ever.'

'To us,' chorused thirty-six staff, quaffing their well-earned drugged champagne.

Five minutes later Reg was having the time of his life. He had removed his wig and wiped the make-up from his face, revealing his eighty-four years with pride. He noted that most of the sleeping celebrities were very heavy on make-up. Some were orange. *And none of them have wrinkles*, he noticed, *not even the old ones. How odd*. He took a small magnifying lens from his pocket and approached a sleeping lady, marvelling at her sparkly necklace. He bent down and snipped it, catching the weight of it in his hand. *Feels heavy*, he thought. *Always a good sign*. He put the small lens to his eye and examined the jewels. 'Nope,' he said, blinking a magnified eye. 'Fake diamonds. That's modern celebrity for you. In my day, film stars would only wear real diamonds. That's another example of standards slipping.'

Reg spent a happy hour examining the celebrities' sparkly jewellery. He'd chosen the job with this night in mind. He was in pursuit of diamonds and it was a fair bet that there would be celebrities dripping with them at an event like this. He was pleased with his evening's work. But the first orange people were beginning to rouse themselves, all woozy-headed, so he thought it best to leave.

His rucksack was satisfyingly heavy. His best haul had come from a young lady whom he'd seen on a daytime soap opera. Two diamond earrings and a marvellous belly-button diamond. *Nice*, he'd thought, easing it out with a toothpick. And he couldn't resist Gordon Blooming-Whittingstall himself. The restaurant owner had been snoring on the floor. Reg had struggled to get the diamond ring off his bloated finger, but he'd applied some of his washing-up liquid and managed it in the end. Plus Gordon's fabulous diamond-encrusted watch. *What a bonus*, thought Reg, popping that into his bag and slipping out into the London night. *The Past Master will be pleased with me*.

5. Great Expectations

The best thing in the world was when the children and animals got to visit Professor Cortex in his lab. But today they'd had to settle for second best, watching as the professor's black van swept on to the drive. He was visiting them.

Ollie jumped down from the sofa and started tearing round the lounge. 'He's here, he's here . . .'

Spy Pups, Spud and Star, were so excited that their whole bodies wagged. Shakespeare watched Lara. *She's what I aspire to be*, thought the cat, learning fast. *Fully qualified secret agent. Baddie-catcher extraordinaire*. He noticed that even the coolest dog on the planet was failing to control her enthusiasm, her tail batting hard against the table, her bullet-holed ear standing higher than ever. *And what a silly doggy grin*, noticed the cat.

Shakespeare was good at noticing things. He observed his newly adopted family with pride and reflected on his first month with them. *Mum seems to be in charge. Dad does as he's told*. At twelve, Ben was the oldest and therefore the leader of the children and Lara seemed to be this little man's best friend. Ollie was the youngest, a whirlwind of innocent trouble, always asking questions and always a whisker away from breaking something.

And then there was Sophie. *My beloved Sophie*, thought Shakespeare, his eyes fixed adoringly on the little girl. He loved her freckles and her warmth. Her grin lit up the room as the white-coated Professor Cortex swept through the door. Ollie hurled himself at the scientist, burying his face in his tummy.

'Quite,' fussed the elderly man, patting Ollie on the head and shaking Ben's hand at the same time.

The professor was, as always, flanked by black-suited, sunglass-wearing minders. Ollie was always intrigued, trying to engage them in conversation when he knew they weren't there to chat. He had no idea what was going on behind their dark glasses, but he could imagine their eyes swivelling right and left, always alert. There was a curly wire sneaking out of the top of Agent P's jacket and into his ear so Ollie knew he was listening. 'Is that an iPod?' asked the little boy, pointing at the wire. 'Have you been downloading?'

Agent P looked straight ahead, his lips sealed.

'Can you speak?'

'Affirmative,' snarled the man from the corner of his mouth.

'Affirmative?' repeated Ollie. 'Cool. That must be a foreign language. Are you from Belgium? Or Swindon? Have you got a gun?'

Ollie thought he saw Agent P twitch. 'And, when you kill baddies, do their guts explode?' he asked, shooting the bodyguard with an imaginary gun.

'Enough questions, Master Oliver,' chirped Professor Cortex. 'Agents P and Q are my personal bodyguards. We go everywhere together.'

'Even the toilet?' gasped Ollie. 'What if there's only one toilet and there are three of you? How does that work?'

'We go *almost* everywhere together, Master Oliver. And do you know why?' He moved on before the little boy had the chance to jump in. 'Because my science experiments are the most advanced in the world. And because the graduates of my Spy School training programme –' he paused, nodding at the wagging dogs – 'are some of the most highly trained secret agents in the world. One can only imagine what would happen if enemy agents got their hands on my technology. Or my brain.' He shuddered. 'Unthinkable.'

Ben considered this rather big-headed so he thought he'd bring the professor down a peg. 'But,' he reminded him, 'some of your inventions are rubbish. That automatic hair-cutter that almost took Dad's head off, for instance.'

Dad was nodding vigorously. 'That was a close shave,' he agreed. 'Literally!'

'Or those pants you invented. The ones that you tested on Agent Q. The ones that were supposed to heat up in the cold and cool down on warm days. The ones that you wired wrong.'

'Well, yes,' agreed the professor, glancing at Agent Q whose body language had sagged a little at the traumatic memory. 'A good idea. Just badly engineered.'

Agent Q shivered. It had taken three days for his private parts to defrost.

'Theory and practice are sometimes different,' suggested the scientist. 'And I have had plenty of successes,' he reminded them, regaining his mojo. 'Plus, I'm pretty sure you'll find some of these rather thrilling.'

The children and dogs crowded round, eagerly awaiting some of Professor Cortex's latest inventions, keen to give them the thumbs-up or down. The professor glanced at Agent Q and was passed a small rucksack. 'This,' he said triumphantly, 'is a little bag of gadgets that I call my Cat Kit.'

Spud grinned a silly doggy grin. 'That sounds like my fave chocolate,' he woofed, slobber dribbling from his chops.

'And I call it a Cat Kit because it's got gadgets aimed at our *newest* secret agent,' the professor said, glancing at Shakespeare. 'The world's finest feline and, I have to say, the world's top ginger secret agent.'

Shakespeare liked it when Lara sometimes called him a ginger ninja. He sat tall, his

translating collar flashing and his eyes shining. *Less chat, Prof*, he thought. *I can't wait to see what's in the Cat Kit*.

'First things first,' began the professor. 'This video will give you a clue. But, before any canines get too excited, this invention is for *cats*. Dogs are simply too heavy,' he noted, glancing at Spud. 'Check this footage of flying squirrels.' He clicked on his laptop and the children gasped as they watched a short sequence of squirrels leaping from trees, spreading their limbs and gliding through the forest.

'Is that for real?' asked Ollie, holding out his arms and pulling at his armpits, hoping to see little wings.

'One hundred per cent real,' nodded the professor, beginning to hop from foot to foot as his excitement mounted. 'These squirrels have evolved. They have loose skin so that when they raise their arms and legs it increases their body surface area. They can't fly as such. They glide. And,' he said, his smile turning into a full-blown beam, 'if we wait four million years, cats might have evolved to do the same. But I've taken a short cut. Basically, I've trimmed evolution by four million years to create this,' he said, pulling a small Lycra suit from his briefcase.

'It looks a bit small for you,' giggled Sophie.

'It's not for humans,' continued the professor. 'It's a catsuit!'

Shakespeare gulped. He felt everyone's eyes turning in his direction. *A what suit?* he thought, patting his translating collar to check it hadn't mistranslated.

'I haven't tested it yet,' admitted the professor. 'But I've run various computer simulations that seem to show it'll work purrrfectly well,' he jabbered. 'Did you see what I did there, Agent CAT? I added an extra-long "urrr" to turn "perfect" into "purrrfect". Because cats . . .'

'We get it, Prof,' sighed Ben. 'If you have to explain your jokes, that basically means they're not funny.'

'Oh,' said the professor, his hopping slowing a little. 'That's a CAT-astrophe. Hey, everyone, I did it again,' he said, missing the point entirely. 'I emphasized the "cat" bit of . . .'

'No,' interrupted Sophie, 'a catastrophe would be strapping poor old Shakespeare into this thing and it *not* working. Poor puss,' she said, running her hand along Shakespeare's back. 'That'd be an awful thing to do.'

Shakespeare was enjoying being fussed over, but he refused to purr. *I agree*, he nodded. *If cats were meant to fly, we'd have feathers!*

'I'll test it,' yapped Spud. 'Is it a bird? Is it a plane? No it's "Super Spud", swooping down and grabbing sweets from children or pies from fat people, making the world a healthier place . . .'

'Please stop the yapping, Agent Spud. Dogs have too much body fat. This is for cats and, from the swishing of the tail, I'm assuming Agent CAT isn't impressed. It's for emergencies only,' assured the professor. 'But you never know. In the world of baddies and spies, sometimes unexpected moments crop up.'

Well, I can't see a moment when I jump off a tall building, swooping through the sky like super-cat, cropping up, thought Shakespeare, swishing his tail to confirm his annoyance. *Although*, he considered, a second thought sneaking into his mind, *how about surprising a few birds by swooping from the rooftop?*

'OK,' said Professor Cortex. 'Let's be a bit more "down to earth".' He quickly glanced around to see if anyone had noticed his clever use of language again. Lara had, shaking her doggy head just enough to show she'd got it, and it was rubbish, so he pressed on.

He pulled a book from his bag. 'Cast your eyes over this, young Oliver,' he said, handing the book to the youngest member of the family. 'It's my greatest invention yet!'

6. *Rocket Science*

'It's a book,' said Ollie matter-of-factly.

'I think you might find they've already been invented,' said Sophie, still upset that the professor could even think about throwing her beloved cat off a tall building.

'Designed to stimulate the olfactory and gustatory senses,' noted the professor, waiting for the inevitable looks of confusion on the children's faces. 'I love reading,' he said, rubbing his hands enthusiastically. 'In fact, what you eventually realize is that all the best people in the world love reading. But traditional books have always stimulated the eyes, ears and hands. What I mean is that you need your eyes to read it, your ears to listen to the words as you read them and your hands to hold it. Books also have a smell, of course, but, as the world moves on and people use electronic books, that smell will die out. A bit of a shame, to be honest.'

'Professor,' sighed Sophie, 'what on earth are you babbling about?'

'I want to enhance the experience of books so you can enjoy them through *all* your senses,' enthused the professor, waving his hands in a volcanic eruption. 'Master Oliver,' he said, grinning over the top of his spectacles, 'what book have I given you?'

Ollie looked at the cover. '*Charlie and the Chocolate Factory*,' he said, holding the book up so everyone could see.

'Then I suggest you turn to page one.'

Ollie did as he was told and a smell of melting chocolate filled the room. 'Wow,' he smiled, 'chocolate!' The little boy flipped through a few pages, letting the aroma waft around the room.

Spud was wagging hard.

'Olfactory means "sense of smell",' explained the professor. 'So *Charlie and the Chocolate Factory* smells of chocolate, bringing life to the book. But that's only half the story,' he continued. 'Gustatory means "sense of taste". Lick a page, young Oliver, or maybe nibble a corner.' He mimicked a mouse nibbling some cheese.

Spud had joined the little boy. *This sounds like my kind of book*, he thought, a bit of drool landing on page six.

Ollie licked a page. 'Yum,' he said, beaming at everyone in the room. 'Choccy flavour.'

Spud couldn't resist; his long tongue slapped on to page six, his eyes spinning in chocolate heaven. Lara cast a warning eye. 'Spud,' she woofed. 'Dogs and chocolate don't mix.'

Ollie had ripped out a page and was chewing it. '*Nom*,' he said. 'It smells *and* tastes of chocolate.'

'Exactly,' grinned the scientist. 'Imagine how many children will want to read my brand-new "sensory stories". Imagine when all books smell and taste, as well as pleasing the eye and ear.'

Ben was licking the book. But he looked unsure. 'So you've invented a book that smells and tastes of chocolate. I'm not sure I get the point.'

'The point, Master Benjamin,' said the professor, rolling his eyes in frustration, 'is that it's not just chocolate. All books can come alive. You can use my invention for any flavour and smell. It doesn't have to be just chocolate. *The Secret Garden* will be roses and fresh air. *James and the Giant Peach* . . .'

'You could make that smell of giants,' interrupted Ollie.

'Or peaches,' corrected the professor. 'That might work better.'

The family were silent for a minute, brains whirring.

Spud was wagging so hard his body was

rocking. *I hope he does a Peppa Pig one*, thought the puppy. *A spicy bacon-flavoured book. Yum!*

'A couple of problems spring to mind,' snorted Sophie. 'First of all, won't kids just eat the books instead of reading them? I don't think a book needs to be a snack.'

'Well, yes,' flustered the professor. 'That is a possibility.'

'And I'd avoid *Winnie the Pooh*,' suggested Ollie. 'That might put children off reading forever!'

'Quite,' smiled the professor. He took a deep breath and puffed out his chest, trying to hide the deflation he felt on the inside. *Maybe I'm too old*, he thought. He cast his mind back to the wonderful inventions of the past. He looked at Spud licking at the chocolate book. *And it's come to this. A chocolate book and a Lycra catsuit*. He shook his head and exhaled, his shoulders sagging. *Rocket science it isn't*.

Eddie put on his extra-magnified spectacles and studied his calculations one last time. 'Rocket science,' he chuckled, 'my favourite subject.' His merry band of ancient volunteers didn't know much about the Past Master. If they'd been able to access the Internet, they would have found out he was a war veteran, aeroplane engineer, scientist and inventor. He was proof that age was no restriction on ideas.

His tweezers rummaged through the small mound of diamonds, searching for the best

one. He chose the largest and dropped it into place. He wasn't just working on an invention. He was planning a revolution. Eddie had spent forty-five years as an engineer and, although his hands were a bit wobbly, his brain was in fantastic shape. He'd started out designing and building aeroplane engines. After the Second World War he'd been part of a top-secret government project that was involved with advanced weaponry. His team had built the world's first laser gun. It sat, unused, in an underground bunker. But the brainpower behind it had been put to very good use.

His team watched as the Past Master checked the drawing on the table in front of him. It showed a detailed diagram of a new type of weapon, something the team knew as the time machine. Eddie chose another diamond, a small one, and fixed it into place.

He looked up at his followers and their faces lit up in matching wrinkly grins. There was a saying: 'you can't teach an old dog new tricks', and it annoyed him greatly. Project GoD was staffed entirely by 'old dogs' and they were going to teach the world a new trick or two.

'The Internet has changed the world,' he told them. 'Destroyed it completely. Everything is so fast, but nobody seems happy.' The Past Master looked out of his office window, the top floor of the Shard, the highest workplace in Europe. London sprawled below, a frantic network of people on the go. His followers followed his pointing finger. 'Eight million fools, rushing around,' he said. 'And that's only what the eye can see. Thousands more, travelling in underground trains, and hundreds up there.' He cast his crooked finger up towards the aeroplanes circling Heathrow, waiting for their turn to touch down.

The Past Master knew that Project GoD was aiming higher than the clouds. He looked up into the evening sky. 'Soon the stars will be twinkling,' he said. 'And that's where we'll be aiming, team. Project GoD, Phase Two. We're ready to go.'

It was dusk, the fading sun reflecting off Western Europe's tallest building. London buzzed below as the Past Master pressed a button and the north-facing roof of the Shard glided open.

The pensioners settled down to watch. 'It doesn't look like a time machine,' suggested Donald, peering through his varifocals. 'I was expecting something like the Tardis.'

The Past Master chuckled. 'That's because nobody's ever invented a time machine,' he explained. 'The Tardis isn't real, Donald. But this is.'

'But wasn't *Doctor Who* better in the olden days?' interrupted Gladys. 'When the Doctor was in black and white.'

'Ooh yes,' agreed Una. 'It's all *crash, bang, wallop* nowadays. I haven't got a clue what's going on. They've even changed the theme tune. And the old Doctor didn't used to have a sonic screwdriver . . .'

'Well, this particular time machine doesn't work like the Tardis,' interrupted the Past Master. 'I've used my intellectual genius to rethink what time machines should look like. So, ladies and gents, quiet, please.'

The old man stood by the contraption. At the bottom it had something that looked like a lawnmower engine. Various pipes and tubes fed upwards to a rotating ball. *Almost exactly like a glittery disco ball*, he marvelled, *except the glittery parts are diamonds*.

His fingers were too arthritic to cross so he made a wish in his head instead. He turned to his elderly audience. 'Energy,' he began.

'I remember that,' rasped Albert from the back.

'The science is simple,' beamed the Past Master. 'Diamonds are the toughest element

on the planet. Almost impossible to destroy. I've been experimenting with heating them to unbelievable temperatures. While most other materials just disintegrate, I've found that diamonds merely keep heating up and that this heat can be focused.' He patted the contraption. 'And, once the energy is focused, it can be directed to a target and that target will go *boom*.'

His audience gasped and Margaret's backside let out a squeak of wind in excitement. 'Whoops, excuse me,' she chuckled. 'Mrs Windy Pops.'

'We've taken out Wales,' continued the Past Master, his brand-new teeth shining too whitely for an eighty-year-old. 'Now it's Scotland's turn to go back in time.' The assembled crowd of old people had fallen silent, their cups returned to their saucers, their tongues and Margaret's backside taking a well-earned rest. This was their moment.

The Past Master knew that timing was everything. Modern communication relied on hundreds of satellites that circled the earth. Eventually his sparkly glitter ball would take out the whole of the European Union, but he'd have to wait for the satellites to be aligned. 'I mean,' he chuntered, as he applied a last squirt of oil to the machine, 'we shouldn't even have joined the European Union in the first place. They keep making us change things! And it's about time we changed them back.'

He knew that Satellite SD6577 beamed data to and from Scotland. He'd nicknamed it the 'McSatellite'. He'd calculated the orbit and knew that it was nearly in range. Scotland was about to lose all satellite communication. *Without McSatellite, Scotland will have no Internet. No mobile phones. No Wi-Fi. No satnav. People will have to slow down. It will force people to talk to each other instead of so-called 'social networking'*. 'Facebook,' he tutted. 'In my day, we didn't have virtual friends, we had real ones. We didn't Tweet, we chatted.' He checked his watch, waiting for the second hand to click to the upright position.

'I hope he hurries up,' whispered Edna. 'I need a wee.'

The second hand ticked into position. 'Now!'

He'd enlisted Barry to help him start the machine. At eighty-one, Barry was one of the younger and fitter members of the Project

GoD team. He yanked the cord and the lawnmower-powered engine spluttered into life. The Past Master adjusted the choke and the machine roared. He smiled at his audience before pressing a big red button and the glitter ball started to glow. He'd calculated that it'd take thirty-six seconds to warm to the correct temperature.

'Soon the intense heat will be magnified by the diamonds at the core and the beam of light will be sufficient to take down the Scottish satellite!'

But his yell was drowned out by the lawnmower engine. The Past Master stepped back as the machine hummed and spluttered. Exactly thirty-six seconds later a narrow beam of light shot into the sky. Precision was everything. The Past Master was confident that, somewhere in space, a satellite had exploded and Scotland had been plunged back in time. He stepped forward and pulled a lever, the machine clunked to a halt, magnifying the silence. His audience looked at him expectantly.

'Is that it?' asked Frank. 'I mean, how do we know if it worked?'

'Trust me, old fellow,' grinned the Past

Master. 'The satellite is down and Scotland is offline. It's been transported back in time. Back to when the world was friendlier and slower. Back to a time when you could leave your back door unlocked. Back to a time when you knew who your neighbours were . . .'

There was enthusiastic cheering from his audience. The Past Master clenched a knuckled fist and punched the air in a silent cheer.

'Project GoD – the "Good old Days" – here we come!'

7. *Hilda and Harold*

It was the Scottish children that noticed it first. 'Mammy,' yelled Alastair, 'I cannie get my Xbox connection to work.'

'OMG, Facebook's down,' yelled fourteen-year-old Moira from her bedroom. 'Nightmare!'

Dad huffed into the kitchen. 'I can't access my work emails,' he complained.

'Well, it's 8 p.m. You shouldn't be looking at work emails anyway,' said Mum, looking up from her laptop. 'Oh bother, I was just watchin' a funny cat video on YouTube and it's frozen.'

Moira came clattering downstairs, shaking her mobile phone. 'Rubbish phone has no signal,' she complained, as if it was her mother's fault.

The family assembled in the kitchen. 'No

Internet,' moaned Dad. 'What on earth are we going to do?'

Agent Q beckoned to Professor Cortex and whispered something in his ear. The scientist looked shocked. 'Are you certain?'

'Affirmative, sir,' he said, tapping his earpiece. 'It happened a few moments ago. Direct from MI6.'

'Good heavens above,' said the professor. He turned to the family and dabbed his brow with a spotty hankie. 'Things are moving faster than I thought,' he said, his white face worrying the children.

'What's up, doc?' asked Ollie. 'You look like you've seen a ghost.'

'You may be aware,' said the professor, tucking his hankie back up his sleeve, 'that Wales went offline a few hours ago.'

Mum, Dad and Shakespeare nodded. Everyone else had been having too much fun to watch the news.

'Well, it seems that Scotland has gone too. The whole country has been blacked out. MI6 has informed me that the satellite has been blown out of orbit. I mean, one minute it was there and the next: *kaboom*,' he explained, reaching for his hankie again. 'Enemy agents for sure. Sharp minds too. This is cutting-edge weaponry. It is very serious indeed.'

'It will be if my Xbox goes offline,' said Ben sternly.

'It's more serious than your Xbox, young Benjamin,' spluttered the professor, failing to hide his irritation. 'It means that Wales and Scotland have been plunged back in time. Back to when computers hadn't been invented. Back to a time before your parents were born.'

'Crikey, back to Victorian times?' gasped Ollie.

'Not quite that far, Master Oliver,' said the professor, casting a weak smile towards Mrs Cook. 'But certainly back to the 1950s or 60s. That'll never do.'

Ben peeked at his mobile phone, reassured that there was still a signal.

The professor looked ashen with worry. 'And I have a horrible feeling that we might be next.'

The Past Master had allocated assignments. Hilda and Harold had been chosen for the most difficult mission. It was also potentially the most rewarding with fifty diamonds on offer. If Hilda and Harold could pull this one off, the plan would be almost complete.

Bank robbers had certain stereotypical characteristics. They were sharp-minded, violent, ruthless, shouty, quick and always dressed in black. Hilda and Harold didn't really fit the bill, although Hilda was a bit shouty (largely because she was hard of hearing) and they were

dressed in black. They'd even gone so far as painting their mobility scooters black especially for this occasion.

Getting into the vault was supposed to be fairly straightforward. It was the getting out bit that was going to be difficult.

The Past Master had organized entry. Their story had been phoned through to the bank manager. She'd been told to expect an elderly couple who would be dressed in black because they'd come straight from a funeral. Their ID had been checked and the security guard had searched Hilda's basket. He'd questioned the need for gas masks, but Harold had explained about Hilda's condition. 'It's an experience my wife had in the war,' he said. 'The Blitz, sonny. Way before your time. If it wasn't for us, you'd be speaking German. Poor Hilda here, she was traumatized as a young girl – *wasn't you, love?* – and can't go anywhere without a gas mask.'

The security guard had raised an eyebrow and attempted to explain that they'd have to leave the basket at reception, so Hilda had done as they'd practised. The old lady started her rapid breathing exercise. 'She's nearly ninety,' explained Harold. 'Dodgy ticker,' he said, tapping his chest. 'Isn't that right, dear? You really don't want to get her worried.'

The security guard looked at the frail old lady and thought better of it. He knew they'd just come from a funeral and didn't want to push things too far. He'd seen movies and he knew bank robbers were young and shouty, not old and breathless. He beeped them through security and followed them, just above snail's pace, down the corridor to the vault where the safety-deposit boxes were kept. Their fake ID had secured them the key to box number 1. The security guard had always wondered what was kept in box number 1.

Harold fumbled with the key. He knew that if he took long enough the security guard would step in and help. And, sure enough, 'Let me get that for you, sir,' he offered. The guard inserted the key, tapped in the number and the door beeped open. By the time he turned round, the old people had their masks on and Hilda had sprayed something in his face. He blinked a couple of times and then hit the floor with a thud.

'I can't hardly see what I'm doing, Harold,' complained the old lady through her mask.

'There's no rush, love,' reassured her partner in crime, his wheezy breathing magnified by the mask. 'He'll be snoozing for a good while.'

Hilda took the diamonds from the safety-deposit box and, one by one, dropped fifty uncut diamonds into her plastic pillbox. She replaced the childproof plastic lid and popped it into her handbag. The elderly couple removed their gas masks and grinned at each other. They'd not had this much fun for seventy years.

Now for the difficult bit. Harold led Hilda by the elbow and they waddled down the corridor. They stood at the security door and waited. They knew the camera would be focused on them and that questions would be asked as to why the guard wasn't with them. The woman on reception did think it was unusual, but she knew their story. The old couple, dressed in black, had come straight from a funeral. She thought about her own grandparents, much younger than this frail couple . . .

It seemed like an age before the door buzzed and Harold pushed it open with his walking stick. They waved to the lady on reception and inched their way into the cold evening air. Hilda's heart was racing. She was sure she'd need her pills when she got home. If she got home! She climbed aboard her mobility scooter, waiting patiently for her accomplice to board his getaway vehicle.

Inside the bank the vault door had been opened and the security guard discovered, sleeping like a baby. The alarm sounded and people started rushing around. Outside, Hilda's hearing aid picked up the sound of police sirens drifting through the streets. Her heart rate quickened to dangerous levels. Dozens of cars were descending on them in a high-speed chase. Hilda led the getaway, Harold in her slipstream. Maximum speed was 4 mph, but that was fast enough for the jet-black mobility scooters to melt into the darkness of the streets.

8. A Plan, of Sorts

The family watched as Professor Cortex paced round the garden, his mobile stuck to his ear. He was wagging his finger at whoever was on the other end and kept shaking his head violently.

'Agent P said it was the primed minister,' said Ollie. 'Whoever it is, it sure looks serious.'

'He's coming,' hissed Sophie as the white-coated scientist marched up the path towards the back door.

'Righty-ho,' announced the professor, bursting through the door. 'There's some serious stuff happening and the PM wants me to sort it out. I've made some arrangements and have got a fantastic opportunity for the family. Mrs Cook,' he said, his smile not entirely convincing, 'how do you fancy a luxury river cruise?' He waited for the information to sink in. 'On the Thames. In London!'

Star and Spud's wags intensified. *Life on the river sounds good!*

Mrs Cook looked a little flustered, her hand patting her chest in excitement. 'Oooh, Professor, or should I say Maximus,' she swooned. 'We've always wanted to go on a cruise. Haven't we, darling?' she said, fluttering her eyelashes at her husband.

'Yes, *you* have,' he reminded her. 'But cruises are just full of old people. I'm not sure it's really our thing.'

'Oh, you're so out of date, Mr Cook,' scolded the professor. 'And besides this wouldn't be just any old cruise. It'd be aboard the *TriTanic*, the most luxurious boat in the world.'

'Cool,' cooed Ben. 'I've read about it. It's brilliant, Dad. It's usually moored in Monte Carlo. And the prof's right. It's not for old people at all. The *Tri*'s got a restaurant and even an amusement arcade.'

'Amusement arcade!' Ollie pretended to faint, falling on to the sofa in excitement.

Spud had stopped listening at the 'restaurant' bit, already planning his meals. *If it's all inclusive*, he thought, *I can have a full English, mid-morning muffins, then lunch and afternoon tea. Then there'd be a little bit of room for an evening meal and late-night supper too! Ooh, and I could sneak some cheese back to my room for a midnight snackeroony*.

Dad was floundering a bit. It seemed OK, but he wasn't convinced he was the cruising type. 'Sounds expensive,' he said. 'I doubt we could afford it, especially if it's the most luxurious river cruiser in the world.'

'Oh, don't worry about that,' assured the professor. 'It's all paid for. In fact, the tickets are already booked. We're going tomorrow. You two, the children, me . . .' he glanced at Lara and the pups before looking away nervously, '. . . and the, er . . . cat.'

Shakespeare had been listening intently, his flashing collar translating the conversation. He liked the idea of the family going on a river cruise. It'd give him a chance to have the place to himself. He was gently purring as he listened. Until the professor's final sentence . . .

Cat! Shakespeare's claws dug into the sofa as he felt his world falling apart.

'The cat!' yelped Spud. 'You missed us out, Prof,' he woofed, jumping up at the white coat and tugging it with his teeth. 'The cruise ship has a restaurant. I've already planned my meals!'

'Down, Agent Spud,' hissed the professor, swatting at the puppy. 'I know you want to come too. But, quite frankly, it's impossible to get you aboard.'

'Why on earth are we taking the cat?' asked Mum, a note of suspicion rising in her voice.

Very good question, thought Shakespeare, his claws digging deeper. *This cat doesn't do boats because boats are surrounded by water! My worst nightmare. This is non-negotiable.*

'There isn't a catch, is there, Professor? This isn't one of your hare-brained schemes?' asked Mum.

'Mrs Cook, Mrs Cook, Mrs Cook,' sighed the professor, struggling for words. 'I mean Barbara,' he said, attempting a watery smile. 'Hare-brained schemes indeed,' he chuckled, his brain whirring, but his mouth struggling to explain what was clearly a hare-brained scheme. 'Let's all sit down and stay calm.'

'I am sitting down. And I was calm,' snarled Mrs Cook. 'And you've never called me Barbara.'

'Well, Barbara it shall be from now on, Mrs Cook,' gabbled the professor, his scientific brain struggling to find an explanation that would fit the bill. 'Let me explain.'

I think you better had, thought Lara, casting

her eye at Shakespeare who looked absolutely terrified. *The Spy Pups seem keen as mustard, but Spy Cat much less so*.

The professor pressed a key on his laptop and it sprang into life. Everyone, dogs and cat included, crowded round. 'This is top secret, OK?' he warned, a raised eyebrow emphasizing his point.

Mrs Cook's sunny disposition had clouded over. 'It's not a holiday. It's an assignment.

A mission! You're putting us all at risk. Again!'

'Barbara,' smiled the professor. 'Babs . . .'

'Mrs Cook,' rumbled Mum, her frown now thunderous. 'Don't "Babs" me!'

'I'll admit it is a mission,' he said, doing inverted commas in the air, 'of sorts. But there is absolutely zero risk to you or the children. Unless,' he said, breaking into a false smile and a hollow chuckle, 'you think saving the world

and having fun are dangerous.' The professor noticed that nobody else was smiling so he ploughed on. 'It involves a *free* river cruise. Including, let me add, two nights aboard the world's most luxurious vessel. The only potential risk is to Agent CAT.' The professor looked round. 'Speaking of which, where is my newest secret agent?'

Shakespeare had retreated to the window sill, listening intently, eyeing an escape route, but resisting the urge to run.

'Here's my thinking,' explained the professor. 'Two satellites have been shot down. Wales and Scotland are off the grid. I can't be sure of who or how at this stage, but I can hazard a pretty safe guess at evil baddies.'

Spud and Star sat tall, tails swishing and ears pricked at the mention of evil baddies.

'And I've just done some calculations.' He produced a notepad from his coat pocket and everybody's eyes widened as he leafed through pages of diagrams and equations. 'Thermodynamics. There's only one element that could be used to generate enough heat to fire a laser that far.'

All eyes remained wide with expectation.

'Diamonds,' blurted the professor, clicking a button on his laptop that showed a picture of a diamond just in case anyone had forgotten what they looked like. 'Superheated diamonds, that is. And whoever is behind the plot would need hundreds of them.'

The professor hit another laptop key and a picture of Gordon Blooming-Whittingstall appeared on the screen.

'I doubt this is a coincidence,' he explained. 'As we know, there has been a series of crimes – diamond robberies to be specific. All have taken place when rich people have congregated together. This chap is a famous restaurateur. He held a celebrity night when the great and the good enjoyed a meal at Numero Uno. Someone, well, this person to be precise,' noted the professor, clicking to a picture of washer-upper Reg, 'spiked their drinks and made off with a million pounds' worth of sparklers.'

'Crikey, he's a bit old,' remarked Ollie.

'Exactly. We're beginning to identify an interesting pattern.'

Shakespeare was still on the window sill, ears pricked. His senses still told him to run. *Me, near water? He's not just a scientist. He's a mad scientist!* But his new-found sense of adventure meant he'd love to be part of an official mission. He decided to listen a little longer. *Let's hear the professor out*, he thought. *And see what my role is*.

Professor Cortex clicked again and a picture of a train appeared. 'This, folks, is the Orient Express. The most famous and most expensive train in the world. And, last week, guess what? Drinks were spiked and someone made off with a massive hoard of diamonds. Please note,' he said gravely, peering over the top of his spectacles at the breathless family, 'valuables like gold and cash, which could easily have been taken, weren't. Full wallets were left untouched. It's clear that these robbers are only after one thing.'

'Diamonds,' piped up Ben, catching on quickly.

'And you said "robbers",' said Sophie. 'Plural. As though you know there's more than one.'

'Well, here's the thing, young lady,' explained

the professor. 'CCTV pictures have captured several of the villains. And they're all, you know . . .'

'No,' said Sophie. 'We don't.'

'Old people,' blurted the professor. 'And I mean really old people. Not old like me. Old as in ancient.'

'Wow,' gasped Ollie, as if being older than the professor was stretching his imagination.

The professor clicked again and his laptop beamed another picture, this time of an elderly couple dressed in black. 'These two,' he said, 'got away with ten million pounds' worth of diamonds from a high-security safety-deposit box. In a high-security bank!'

'No way!' said Ollie, looking at the couple and sounding impressed. 'Ancient! The oldest bank robbers in the world. How come they haven't been caught?'

'That, Master Oliver, is a very good question. There is a massive reward for their capture. And I mean massive. It would fund my Spy Pet programme for an entire year. But I have a hunch that it's about more than diamond robberies. I think the diamond robberies and the shooting down of satellites are somehow linked.'

Mrs Cook was looking confused. 'I don't get it,' she said. 'What's this got to do with us going on the *TriTanic*?'

'Because, Mrs Cook,' said the professor, his eyes lighting up again, 'there are lots of rich people aboard. With diamonds.'

'So you think the thief will be on-board,' gasped Ben, punching the air in excitement. 'And you're going to capture them and collect the reward.'

'And save the world from going offline,' beamed Ollie.

'Plus, all the robbers are octogenarians,' explained the professor. 'So they're not dangerous.'

'Octogenarians?' asked Ollie.

'Very old people,' volunteered Sophie. 'Like, in their eighties.'

'And do they have eight arms?' asked Ollie, intrigued.

'Pass me tomorrow's newspaper, Agent Q,' said Professor Cortex. 'I've created this,' he said, wafting it in the air.

Shakespeare saw his picture on the front page and became very interested. He hopped down from the window sill and took up a better position.

The professor spread the paper on the table and the family gasped at the front-page headline: **Millennium Diamond Goes Cruising**, and there, centre stage, was a Photoshopped picture of Shakespeare with a massive diamond attached to his collar.

Sophie grabbed the paper and read it aloud. '*Zillionaire Maximus Rich and his cat Shakespeare will be mixing in public for the first time in ten years.*'

'That's me,' said Professor Cortex proudly, before mouthing the rest of the story that he'd written, word for word.

'The recluse and his cat are inseparable. It will be a rare opportunity to view the Millennium Diamond, the world's largest gem, which is traditionally worn around the cat's neck.' Sophie was drawing everyone in with her wide-eyed excitement. 'Maximus Rich declined to give an interview, but issued this statement: "The cruise leaves tomorrow and,

should anyone be interested, I will be in cabin eight." '

'And Bob's your uncle,' sang the professor. 'That's a clear message to the diamond thieves. They know where I am, when I am, and they'll be unable to resist attempting to snatch the precious stone. It's a genius plan . . . *wham, bingo, kazam* . . . caught red-handed. We have ourselves some evil villains.'

'And a way of finding the laser,' said Ben. 'It does sound rather exciting. And we do have the diamond,' he said, recalling one of Lara's previous adventures. 'We kind of kept it.'

'Two questions,' began Mum, not wanting to pass up on the idea of a totally free holiday. 'What's the danger level?'

'Nil, Mrs Cook,' promised the professor. 'A big fat zilcho. None of the other robberies have involved any violence. The pattern has been very predictable. The thief, or thieves, administers a sleeping potion.'

'And why the cat? I mean, Lara is your trusted companion. You and she have solved dozens of crimes. And now you've chosen Shakespeare.'

'It's a decision that's been made for me,' explained the professor. 'Dogs just aren't allowed on-board. Simple as that. But we do need one of the spy team to take the strain. Just in case things do get a little hairy,' he smiled, loving the pun. 'And, in the olden days, there was always a ship's cat. It was useful on long voyages. The ship's cat caught rats and mice. So I've been able to persuade the captain that I can bring Agent CAT. It's the perfect way to advertise the diamond, hanging from the collar of the official "ship's cat".'

Sophie clicked her fingers under the table, beckoning her beloved Shakespeare. The cat's mind was all over the place. He wanted to be an official spy. He was desperate to go on a mission. *But there's no way I can go aboard a boat*.

Lara watched Shakespeare's body language. *Crikey*, thought the Spy Dog. *He looks like a broken puss*.

The family dispersed in excitement. There were bags to be packed and then they had to be up early to drive to London for the trip of a lifetime.

The pups were desperately disappointed not to be going, but they wagged excitedly at Shakespeare. 'You're one lucky puss,' woofed Spud. 'A luxury river cruise, with unlimited food.'

'On the Thames,' barked Star. 'In the most

awesome city on the planet. And the chance to catch a diamond thief!'

Shakespeare tried to look positive, but it was beyond him. His desire to be a qualified spy was overwhelmed by his phobia of water.

His whiskers sagged. Tonight he would be running away from home.

9. Runaway

Shakespeare was heartbroken. *I knew I shouldn't have got too close, too involved with a family*, he thought, *not after last time.*

He cast his mind back to waking up on the riverbank, soggy and half drowned. He lay there and mewed, hoping his mum or brothers and sisters would hear. *But, assuming they survived, his brothers and sisters were all on the other side of the river*. Shakespeare had been tiny and alone. And, even worse, unwanted. He forced himself to his feet. *I think I know what it means to be 'weak as a kitten'*, he thought and stumbled towards the road. A car horn blared. He had walked as far as his tiny kitten feet would take him before he curled up, too weak to go any further.

The river. Water. Horrible, horrible wet stuff. I hate water! If the professor wants me to be a ship's cat, on a boat, he can think again. It's never going to happen. I've nearly drowned once and it's put the 'scared' into 'scaredy cat'.

Shakespeare wasn't sure how it happened, but he assumed someone must have handed him in to a rescue shelter. *Then some nice humans nursed me back to health. And I was adopted by a family with a lovely little girl. She was small. I was small. We were a perfect match. Those were good months. But*, considered Shakespeare, *I must be the unluckiest cat in the world because there was a scuffle with the family dog, my claws caught one of the adults and that was it. I was abandoned again!*

He looked at Sophie, fast asleep. He loved her long eyelashes and freckled cheeks. He looked at the indentation in the duvet. *Probably still warm*, thought the cat, forcing himself to be strong. Running away was tough. But spending time on a boat was tougher. *No more families for me. It always ends in heartbreak.*

Shakespeare took a pencil in his mouth and tapped a brief message for Sophie.

Will MISS u little girl. But I have to go it
Alone. This cat isn't cut out to be a spY.
Will love you 4ever. Please don't be SAd.

Shakespeare wiped a paw across his face. Cats can't cry, but they can feel very sad indeed. He held his paw on the 'x' button until about fifty kisses had been added. *And I mean every single one of them*, he thought.

He checked himself in the mirror. His translating collar was flashing. *That's my passport to a successful future*, he thought. *No more falling in love with kind children. No more being stroked. No more attachment*. He made for the bedroom door and glanced back at the sleeping little girl. His heart was heavy, but his mind made up. *I hope her heart doesn't hurt as much as mine*.

It was as he looked back that Lara made her move. She was a highly trained superspy, a lethal weapon. Her paw came down on Shakespeare's head with just the right amount of force and the cat slumped to the floor.

Shakespeare woke, his vision blurred and his head heavy. The room seemed to be moving. He shook himself awake and looked around, his vision righting itself. He was lying on a bed, in a small room, unlike any room he'd ever been in. He tried to piece the clues together, but they made no sense. *Why on earth has the room got round windows? How odd.*

Shakespeare got to his feet and shook himself to full alertness. He jumped off the bed. *Woah, still swaying*, he thought. *I'm still a groggy moggy. But where am I? And why are my legs so wobbly?*

The Spy Cat jumped silently on to the desk and stretched his neck to peer out of the round window. *Blue sky and blue water*! All of a sudden the clues fitted together. *My legs aren't wobbly. The boat is wobbly. Someone's clonked me on the head and smuggled me on to a ship!* He strained his neck even higher. *River! Water! I'm surrounded by water!*

Shakespeare struggled with his emotions. Anger was high on the list. Along with fear and betrayal. Who on earth had smuggled him on to this boat? His cat's eyes scanned for more clues. The professor's laptop was on the desk with a yellow Post-it note. 'Play me,' read Shakespeare, his translating collar working extra hard to decipher the spidery pen-in-the-mouth writing. The cat pressed the Return key and a home-made video sparked into life. Shakespeare nearly fell off the desk in surprise. It was Lara.

'Hello, Shakespeare, or should I say Agent CAT,' woofed the dog. 'Apologies that you're having to hear this message from the boat's cabin, but I feared that you would never be persuaded aboard . . .'

Too right, thought the cat.

'In fact, I was worried that your fears might even drive you from the home – and people – you love.'

Shakespeare calmed a little. He felt a bit ashamed of his plan to run away from home. *And Sophie in particular*.

'Because, Agent CAT, what has become clear is that, in the short time you've been with us, we've grown very fond of you. Sophie in particular. As the family guardian, I don't want you breaking her heart.'

Or her mine, thought the cat, swishing his tail in regret.

'And,' continued the video, 'we must all learn to confront our deepest fears. In fact,' woofed Lara, gazing seriously into the wobbly camera, 'it is when we confront our deepest fears that we find out who we truly are. So, Agent CAT, I had no choice but to force you aboard. You will find the professor and the Cook family having fun on board the *TriTanic*. But, before you join them, you must wear the collar that you will find in the professor's brief-case. The diamond will put you in peril. We believe the diamond thief is on board and will attempt to steal the gem. Your mission, and you have no choice but to accept it, is to help Professor Cortex to catch the criminal.' Lara left a dramatic pause. 'Or *criminals*. We are very much hoping that we might also be able to stop any more satellites being shot down.'

Shakespeare had gone from terrified to excited. *It does sound kind of cool*, he thought. *I love the idea of keeping an eye on the passengers and working out who the baddie is.*

Lara's woof lowered to an even more serious level and her sticky-up ear rose to full alert. 'But, Agent CAT, you have a more important task. You must keep the children from danger. We call it "rule number one" and it's really all that matters.'

Shakespeare felt a shiver run down his spine.

'So, Agent CAT, we are relying on you, your skills and your bravery. A chance to prove yourself on a double mission – solve the crime AND keep the children safe. Over and out.'

Lara saluted the wobbly camera and Shakespeare heard Star woofing, 'Nice one, Mum, it's in the can,' before Spud's face leered at the screen and he pulled a silly doggy grin as the video cut to black.

Shakespeare sat tall and proud. He tried to

think logical thoughts. *It's a two-day river cruise. And yes, I'm surrounded by water, but the boat's not going to sink.* Shakespeare knew the vessel was carrying 150 passengers. 'One of them is an evil baddie,' he purred. 'Watch out – here I come.'

The cabin door opened and Ben walked in. 'Hi there, puss,' he said. 'Good to see you're awake. I'm assuming you've seen Lara's vid? In which case you'll know the mission. And you'll be needing some help to slip into this.' He pulled the diamond necklace from the professor's bag.

Shakespeare gulped. *That's a whopper!* He stretched his neck as Ben clipped it in place.

'Remember,' said the boy, 'you belong to the reclusive Maximus Rich. The professor's already made himself known. He's quite enjoying himself, playing the eccentric multi-zillionaire. It gives him a chance to be even more bonkers than normal. Come on, puss, let's go bag ourselves a diamond thief.'

10. Maude Aboard

The Shard stands out on the capital's skyline. Its tip is a gleaming focal point of steel and glass, the tallest and most modern of London's buildings.

Yet, on the inside, it was 1950. The top floor was inhabited entirely by pensioners. The floor had a patterned carpet, to hide the dirt. Portraits of royalty looked down on proceedings. Everything was last millennium. And that was exactly the point.

To be part of this elite group you had to be able to remember the war. It didn't really matter which war: any world war would do. The essential ingredient was that these people had been recruited, mostly from old people's homes, with one thing in common: life was better in the olden days.

The Past Master looked around proudly at his team. Some of the ladies were knitting and chatting. There was a small TV in the corner and some of the team had an eye on that. It was a programme about family trees and they loved that kind of thing. Not the new kind of thing. They all agreed that too many TV programmes were rude or just plain loud. 'When our machine gets working, we'll be back to just three TV channels, like in the olden days,' said Iris, her knitting needles clicking reassuringly.

'Oh goody,' said Joan. 'Of course, in the really old days, we didn't have a telly, you know. We just had books.'

'And our imaginations,' sighed Iris.

'And rickets,' remembered Gladys, joining in from the other side of the room. 'My dad says that, during the war, he always left his back door open.'

'That's probably why his submarine sank, Gladys,' offered Iris, glancing up from her knitting.

Geoffrey was brewing the tea. There was always tea available and they made sure it was proper tea, strong and sugary. Not newfangled herbal tea. Theirs was tea from a teapot, made with tea leaves and a tea-strainer. Dot had made a cake and Frank was passing the mints around. And the Past Master knew that after they'd eaten there'd be a sing-song and a game of Scrabble. But, most importantly, there would be chatter and laughter, and stories of when they'd visited the seaside or worked in a factory. Or down the pit. *Not that there are any pits any more*, he thought. *Or many factories, come to think of it. Everyone works in offices. On computers. But our little GoD project will put a stop to all that.*

He eyed the machine. The tests had gone swimmingly. He looked at the huge map of Europe on the wall. Wales and Scotland already had big red crosses through them. *Two down*, he thought.

He was immensely proud of his creation. And now, instead of one laser, the diamonds had been arranged in such a way that it would shoot multiple beams, taking down dozens of satellites orbiting above Western Europe. The good old days would be returned. He imagined receiving his knighthood for 'services to society'.

There was just one more diamond required and he knew exactly which one. The newspaper was spread out on the table before him, Shakespeare's face leering at him, the diamond hanging heavily from his neck. This was the final piece of the jigsaw: this diamond would power the machine. A European blackout beckoned and, because there was no room for error, the Past Master had sent his best agent.

He wondered how Maude was getting on.

Maude had spotted the cat within five minutes of coming aboard the *TriTanic*. She spent her time observing from a distance. She knew it was important to choose the right moment. The old lady watched Professor Cortex overacting terribly, playing the role of Maximus Rich so well that he'd begun to believe it.

Shakespeare's neck was aching. *It's a real effort keeping it held high, with the weight of the biggest carats in the world! But I'm playing a crucial role in capturing the diamond thief.* He forced his neck upright. *Here's the diamond. Come and get it.*

He'd been determined to keep his cat's eyes peeled. But, by day two, the cruise was coming to an end and Shakespeare was feeling frustrated. He'd stayed alert, on the lookout for evil baddies. The cabaret had a magician who looked a bit shifty. The head chef's eyes were too close together. *But everyone else just seems kind of normal.* Shakespeare had studied the pattern of diamond crimes and the professor's words were ringing in his head. *Old people. All the robbers have been very old indeed.* He noticed there was an awful lot of wealth, which is to be expected on the world's most expensive river cruise, but not any really old people.

It was on the second day that Shakespeare's eyes met Maude's. He knew at once that she was the thief. *She's the oldest person aboard. By a mile! She looks like such a sweet old lady and is therefore the most perfect diamond thief in the world*, he thought. Shakespeare sat on the professor's knee, holding his head extra high as Maude brushed past their table.

'May I join you?' she asked.

'Of course,' smiled the scientist, pulling out a chair and sweeping crumbs off it.

The silver-haired lady and the professor got chatting. 'I'm Maude from cabin five and I've got fifteen cats at home,' she cooed, stroking Shakespeare at every opportunity. 'What a lovely collar,' she purred, rubbing her thumb

over the Millennium Diamond. Shakespeare stiffened.

Professor Cortex was also suspicious, sniffing a diamond thief. 'It's the Millennium Diamond,' he said grandly, using his poshest voice. 'I'm a recluse called Maximus Cort – I mean Maximus *Rich*,' he corrected himself.

'Well, Maximus, why don't I get you and I a little drinky?' suggested Maude, creaking to her feet. 'Let's celebrate the last night of our cruise with a nice glass of bubbly.'

The old lady wobbled off to the bar. Shakespeare looked at the professor. He stared back, his eyes and mouth wide. 'She's the one,' he hissed. 'Did you see the way her beady eyes lit up when she rubbed your collar?'

Shakespeare nodded. He jabbed his paw at the professor's cup. *When she comes back your drink will be drugged. On guard, Prof*, thought the cat. *This mission is warming up nicely.*

'She's coming!' hissed Professor Cortex, as Maude collected her drinks from the bartender and started wobbling back to the table. 'I'll keep her busy, you check her cabin for diamonds, OK?' he said out of the side of his mouth. 'She'll be trying to drug me. But I'm

clever. I'll double bluff.' He tapped the side of his nose, 'then when she's asleep I'll join you in cabin five.'

Shakespeare felt his heart thumping, his tail swishing in excitement. *Sounds like a half-decent plan*. He perched on the professor's knee, waiting for the right moment to disappear and explore Maude's cabin.

The elderly lady tottered back to the table, carrying two tall glasses. The professor was the world's best scientist, but wasn't really spy material. While his brain could conjure some magical inventions, it struggled to think under pressure.

Slowly and deliberately, Maude placed one glass in front of the professor and the other in front of herself. She eased back into her seat. 'You look warm, Maximus,' she said. 'You're sweating.'

Professor Cortex took a hankie from his top pocket and mopped his brow. He was doing his best. He couldn't quite bring himself to believe that this lovely old lady was a diamond thief. 'You like diamonds, don't you, Maude?' he blurted, staring into her eyes and trying not to blink.

'I do,' smiled Maude. 'They say that diamonds are a girl's best friend.'

'I bet you have quite a collection.'

Maude smiled a knowing smile. 'You know, don't you?' she said, a twinkle in her eighty-four-year-old eyes. 'And you're not a recluse, are you, Maximus?'

'And you're not a normal passenger, are you,

Maude?' said the professor, calm on the outside but panicking on the inside.

Shakespeare gulped. His heart was racing. *This must be what humans mean when they talk about a cat-and-mouse game*. His ears were on the conversation, but his eyes were on the drinks. *The pattern of the diamond robberies is always the same. The old lady has obviously spiked the prof's drink with a sleeping potion*. He looked at the glasses, bubbles rising. *She knows the professor is on to her. The only thing she doesn't know is that I'm a secret agent cat, ready to pounce. But, as far as the diamond thief is concerned, I must behave like an ordinary mog*.

Shakespeare sat on the professor's knee and purred, trying to look like he imagined an ordinary cat would. Neither of the humans touched their drinks. Maude reached over and tickled Shakespeare behind the ear. 'What a fabulous ship's cat you've been,' she cooed. 'I see you've got two collars. A flashing one and a diamond one. How wonderful.'

Professor Cortex's face was getting redder. He reached for his hankie and mopped again. 'I know about you, Maude,' he blurted. 'And your little caper, and now *you* know I know.

And me knowing you know I know makes things a little . . . you know . . . complicated,' he smiled, losing track of what he was on about.

Maude looked confused. 'You seem to know an awful lot, Maximus. All I know is that I'd like to propose a toast,' she suggested, looking at the champagne glasses.

The professor imagined himself to be one step ahead. 'Here's another thing I know, Maude,' he babbled, pointing at a London landmark behind the old lady. 'There's the Shard,' he said. 'London's highest building. It's so modern and striking. You really must *look*.' His plan was to distract her so that he could swap his drugged champagne for her not-drugged one.

But Maude had been hand-picked for this mission. She didn't *think* she was one step ahead of the professor, she absolutely *knew* she was. Shakespeare held his breath as she turned slowly and surely, giving the professor just enough time to switch the drinks.

Now he had the drugged one.

Phew! Nice move, Prof, thought Shakespeare, not suspecting a thing.

He winked at the cat. 'Shoo,' he mouthed. 'Go and search her cabin.' He jabbed a finger towards the other end of the boat. 'I'll be there in a minute or two.'

'It is rather magnificent,' smiled Maude, turning back to the professor. 'I've heard that the view from the top is something special.'

The professor mopped his brow again, but was grinning broadly. Shakespeare dropped silently to the floor. He heard the champagne glasses clinking, and the gentle conversation continued as he sloped off to cabin number 5.

11. Top Cat

Shakespeare had no trouble finding a way into cabin number 5. The porthole had been left conveniently open. *Too conveniently?* He jumped on to Maude's bed and did a bit of snooping. It was evening time and darkness was settling over London. The cat couldn't reach the light switch so was using his night-vision as best he could. Shakespeare's heart was racing. *This is soooo exciting. A proper mission.* He was sure Professor Cortex would be joining him, just as soon as Maude had sipped her own sleeping potion and was fast off.

The cat checked all the places a cat could. *Under the bed. Clear. On top of the wardrobe. Nothing. I hope the prof hurries up*, he thought. *His hands will be able to make light work of searching in the drawers and cupboards. There has to be a big stash of diamonds somewhere.*

Shakespeare's ears twitched as he heard footsteps shuffling along the corridor. *At last*! He yowled loudly. 'In here, Prof.'

The cat came to full alertness when he heard the scratching sound of a key card being inserted in the door. A dark figure entered the cabin. Shakespeare meowed again. *About time*, he thought. *This place is spooky on my own. We've got diamonds to find.*

Maude was an expert on cats. She had spun the professor a web of lies that contained just one truth: she did have fifteen cats of her own. Shakespeare hissed as he was expertly plucked from the bed, the old lady grasping him firmly by the scruff of the neck.

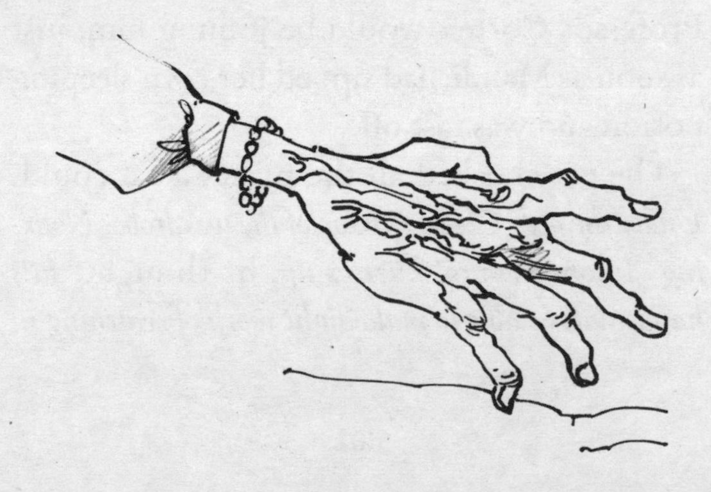

He yowled and hissed again, his claws outstretched and his legs kicking in the darkness. Maude was a sprightly eighty-four-year-old and he was unceremoniously bundled into a bag, the zip sealing him in.

Shakespeare was in a panic. His mind was flooded with thoughts of the last time he was dumped in a bag. *I hate bags. And water. And diamond thieves. And now I hate old ladies too. Let me out!*

Nobody heard his muffled yowling as he was carried on to the top deck. But Maude was on a mission too. There was no way she was going to let the cat out of the bag. The pensioner was alone on the top deck. She took a small torch from her handbag and gave three flashes

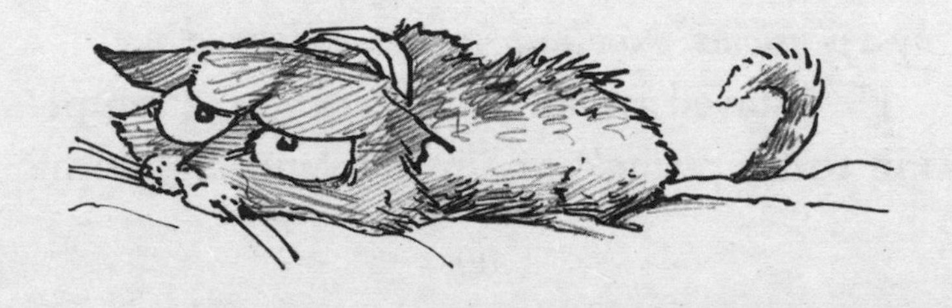

towards Westminster Bridge. The cruise boat sailed on, the lights of the central London riverbank lighting the scene. As the boat passed under the bridge, Maude raised the cat bag above her head. A hook attached to the end of a long piece of rope caught it and the bag left her hands, hauled upwards by Ernest and Albert.

Maude returned to the lower deck, her part of the mission accomplished. She let herself back into cabin 5 and got into her nightie. The professor was fast asleep in the bar. The Cook family had bedded down for the night.

Everyone was going to have a good night's sleep. Except Spy Cat. He crouched in the darkness of the bag, hoping someone would hear his muffled yowls for help. He felt himself being hauled across London and then upwards, to somewhere very high indeed.

This mission has gone from warm to red-hot!

Shakespeare had been left in the bag. He was furious with himself. *Catnapped! Double-crossed by a pensioner. Not quite what we planned.*

He'd stayed awake in the darkness, attempting to keep track of time. Eventually some light crept through the tiny holes in the zip so he assumed it was sunrise. He crouched low as he heard muffled voices. 'You're going to have to be quick, Lenny,' he heard someone say. All of a sudden the zip was ripped apart and a man's bony fingers expertly pinned him down. Another man used a pair of wire-cutters to snip through Shakespeare's diamond collar. Shakespeare struggled and hissed, but to no avail. The diamond collar fell away and the cat struggled until the pressure was released and he flew across the room, hair raised, ready to do battle.

At least my translating collar is intact, he thought, seeking refuge under a table.

'He's just frightened,' he heard a lady say. 'Let's find a saucer of milk. He'll be fine when he settles in. And, when this escapade is all over, he can come home with me.'

Settle in? Come home with you? I'm not planning on either, madam! I've got a perfectly good home with a family I love.

Shakespeare peeped out from under the table. *Old people. Everywhere.* His eyes were drawn to the man who had his diamond collar. He clamped the collar in a vice, slipped a dark mask over his eyes and took a burning flame to it. Before long the diamond fell away from the collar and the man removed the mask. He picked up the diamond in a gloved hand and held it to the light.

'The final piece,' he announced to the room full of old people. 'This day will go down in history. When the satellites align at midday today, we will be going back to the good old days.'

There was a warm round of applause from the old folks.

The good old days? thought Shakespeare. *Old people, diamonds and satellites?* He remembered the professor's theory that the three were somehow linked. His paw went to his translating collar. He felt calmed by the flashing light. He knew that his translating collar also had a tracking device. He thought of the family waking up and realizing their cat was missing. *Help will be on its way*, he thought. *I will infiltrate the gang and pick up a few clues. Eyes and ears alert.*

He jumped effortlessly on to a kitchen table. A man stroked him and a woman laid down a saucer of milk. *No thanks*, he thought. *I'm here to spy.*

'Shush,' hissed one of the old men. 'We're on the news.'

The TV was turned up full volume as the newsreader looked gravely at the camera. 'Panic has set in across Scotland,' he announced. 'We are unable to bring you any pictures because all communication channels are down. Reports indicate that there is no Internet and that TV and radio connections have also failed. There are reports of people getting terribly lost because their satnavs have stopped working and they no longer have the ability to read a map.'

'We didn't have satnav in the war,' Reg pointed out, 'and we never got lost once.'

'But you did bomb the wrong town, dearest,' reminded Ivy.

The news item continued, but Shakespeare's attention was drawn to the map. *Scotland is crossed out? And they said 'we're on the news'?*

He looked down at a huge piece of paper that was unfurled on the table. His translating collar allowed him to unscramble the words and pictures. *It's a diagram of that machine*, he thought, glancing at the contraption that sat in the middle of the floor. There were masses of calculations that he couldn't understand. His eyes fell on a sentence that had the word 'precision' underlined and one that he had to read twice. 'When the machine is started, there will be thirty-six seconds before the lasers ignite.'

Shakespeare was puzzled. His brain was working on an idea that he didn't think was possible. *Especially not by old people. But I suspect I'll have thirty-six seconds to save the world.*

12. Room with a View

The morning sun glittered on the Thames. The plan was for the family to enjoy breakfast on board the boat and then do some sightseeing in the capital city. Mum and Dad had a lie-in so Ben, Sophie and Ollie skipped into the restaurant, only to find Professor Cortex slumped at the breakfast table, snoring like a tractor.

'He's been here all night,' explained the waiter. 'He must have got very drunk.'

'He doesn't really drink,' said Sophie, picking up his empty champagne glass and sniffing it.

Ben slapped the professor on the back. Then again, much harder, and the old man grunted. 'Prof,' he said, aware that the other diners were looking their way, 'it's morning.'

The professor raised his head from the table,

a piece of last night's pepperoni stuck to his cheek and the pattern of a napkin imprinted on his forehead. 'What morning?'

'Our final morning. Before we go sightseeing,'

said Ollie enthusiastically. 'And it looks like there was no diamond thief.'

'You look terrible,' remarked Sophie. 'Where's Shakespeare?' She lifted the tablecloth and looked under the table.

The professor's head hit the table once more and he groaned. 'Oh dear. She's cleverer than I thought. I think something terrible has happened to Agent CAT,' he announced into the tablecloth.

Shakespeare wasn't sure how to play it. The diamond collar had been removed from his neck, but his translating one was still intact. He'd spent ten minutes sulking under a table, hissing at the pensioners. But he'd cleared his head and come to his senses. *What would a Spy Cat do? I need information.*

He'd peeped from his hiding place and had counted fifty-five old people, mostly sitting in comfy armchairs, chatting or doing crosswords. One group of old ladies was engrossed in a jigsaw. A couple of elderly gentlemen were gluing model aeroplanes together. Maude, the old lady who had snatched him, was brewing some fresh tea.

None of them look very dangerous, thought Shakespeare. *I have a big advantage over them. They don't know that I'm a ginger ninja. They don't know that I've got a translating collar. I can be the professor's eyes and ears. I'm sure my family will have noticed I'm missing and are on their way. A Spy Cat would mingle, eyes peeled and ears alert. A Spy Cat would find out what the plot is. I've heard them talking about 'Mission GoD' which is taking place at midday today.*

Shakespeare glanced at the grandfather clock ticking loudly in the corner.

8 a.m. Exactly four hours to save the world.

Sophie was the one who'd brought the professor to his senses. Three strong black coffees had dilated his pupils and his brain was groggy but functioning. 'We are going to find my cat,' she ordered. 'And we're going to find him now.'

All of a sudden the professor could see Sophie as a young Mrs Cook. Resistance was futile. He nodded wearily. Sophie had rummaged in his pockets and found his mobile. 'His translating collar,' she reminded him, 'has a tracking device. So track him!'

Professor Cortex stabbed at a few buttons

and a map appeared. 'Agent CAT is close,' he said, a note of surprise rising in his voice. 'Within half a mile in fact. That way.' He pointed across the river. 'But it's very strange,' he said, shaking his mobile to see if he could get a different reading.

'What's so strange, Professor Calamity?' urged Sophie.

'Agent CAT is three-hundred metres above sea level.'

'On a plane?' panicked Sophie. 'Someone's catnapped poor old Shakespeare and they're flying him out of the country!'

'No, Sophie,' said the professor, looking at the tracking device and shaking his head. 'Agent CAT isn't moving. He's three-hundred metres in the air, that-a-way.' The scientist turned and pointed towards the red dot. The children followed the line of his finger.

He was pointing at the Shard.

13. No Lives Left?

The children had decided not to ask Mum and Dad. 'They'll just say no,' decided Sophie, 'and "no, you can't go and rescue Shakespeare from the diamond thief" is absolutely the wrong answer.'

They had marched the confused scientist off the boat and along the Thames embankment. Ben had Googled 'the Shard' and was checking the details on his mobile phone. 'Viewing platform on level seventy-two. But there are eighty-seven floors. Wikipedia says the top two floors are residential,' he read. 'But it doesn't say who owns them. Three-hundred metres. That must be the very top floor.'

Sophie led the way. She marched forward, a frown fixed on her freckled face. Ben, Ollie and the professor scampered behind.

'Soph,' yelled her big brother. 'We need a plan.'

'I've got a plan,' she thundered, marching faster. 'I'm going to the top of that building to rescue my cat.'

The small gang approached the foyer. A guard in a peaked cap looked them up and down. 'We've got a booking at one of the restaurants,' fibbed the professor, regaining some composure. 'Me and my, erm, kids?'

'Your name, sir?' asked the guard, his eyes scanning a computer screen.

'His name is Professor Cortex,' snorted Ollie. 'And we're here to get to the top floor to rescue our cat. It's all of our's cat really, but Sophie's the most. We've got some dogs too,' he offered, smiling. 'But they couldn't come to London because we've been on a boat and so we only brought our puss. We've tracked him down to here. Well, up there actually.' Ollie pointed his finger skywards. 'He's got a translating collar, you know.'

The professor saw that the security guard was confused. 'We're here for Shakespeare,' he explained.

'Then you'll need a theatre, sir,' advised the

guard, feeling one of his headaches starting to pound.

'If you could just let us up to the top floor, we'd be very grateful,' said Professor Cortex, pressing a £20 note into the guard's hand.

The man pocketed the crisp twenty. All of a sudden he looked interested. 'The top floor, sir,' he said, 'is out of bounds. It's reserved. To be honest, sir, even I don't know what goes on up there. But there have been some strange goings-on,' he confided, lowering his voice.

'Such as?' asked the professor, rummaging in his wallet for another £20.

The security guard waited for the note to land in his palm before continuing. 'The top two floors, sir,' he said, 'are residential. The most expensive apartments in the world.'

'And with the best view,' suggested Professor Cortex, attempting to hurry the man along. 'So what kind of *strange* goings-on?'

Another £20 was pocketed. 'There's a special lift that goes up to the very top floors, sir. Highly restricted access. I've never been up there personally. I can only go as far as the restaurant, that's the thirty-third floor. But there have been a lot of people using the private lift. Strange people, if you know what I mean?'

Sophie's cat had been abducted and she couldn't wait any longer. She snatched the professor's bulging wallet and wafted it in front of the security guard's wide eyes. 'What kind of strange people? We want to get up there.'

The little girl waved the wallet around and the man's eyes tracked it, like Spud did with a chocolate éclair.

'Old people,' he said, mesmerized by the chunky wallet. 'Loads of very old people. They go up and they never come back down. A community of pensioners.'

'There, told you,' said Sophie, turning to the others. 'Shakespeare has been catnapped by a bunch of evil diamond thieves who just happen to be pensioners. And somehow they're intending to destroy the Internet. It makes perfect sense.'

'It does?' asked the guard, his eyes still on the professor's fat wallet.

'Get us up there,' ordered Sophie.

'I c-can't,' stammered the guard, fearing his easy cash bonus would disappear before his very eyes.

'Can't or won't?' frowned Sophie.

'I can only get you as far as the restaurant,' he said. 'After that, you'd have to take the, ahem, secret stairs.'

In pride of place, in the middle of the room, sat a strange-looking contraption. Shakespeare eyed it curiously. *The bottom half looks like the lawnmower that Dad keeps in the shed. And then there's a series of pipes and tubes. And what on earth is that sparkly thing swinging above it?* He cast his mind back to the school disco when he'd popped by to fetch Sophie. *It looks like a glittery disco ball,* he thought, remembering the one that had been suspended from the school ceiling. *How odd. Maybe the old people are going to be doing some disco dancing.* Shakespeare gulped as the realization hit him. *The glittery things on the disco ball are diamonds!*

A man was kneeling next to the contraption. He had opened the panel on the lawnmower and seemed to be fixing the diamond – *my diamond* – inside. He closed the panel and dusted his hands together. 'Precision engineering,' he announced. 'Everything is sorted, right down to the last thousandth of a millimetre. The satellites are nearly aligned. Our time is coming.'

Shakespeare hoped his family were tracking him through his translating collar. He glanced at the grandfather clock ticking its way past 11.30 a.m. *Whatever's going to happen is going to happen soon!* Shakespeare's previous scrapes had used up a few of his nine lives. *I just hope I've got enough left to save the world.*

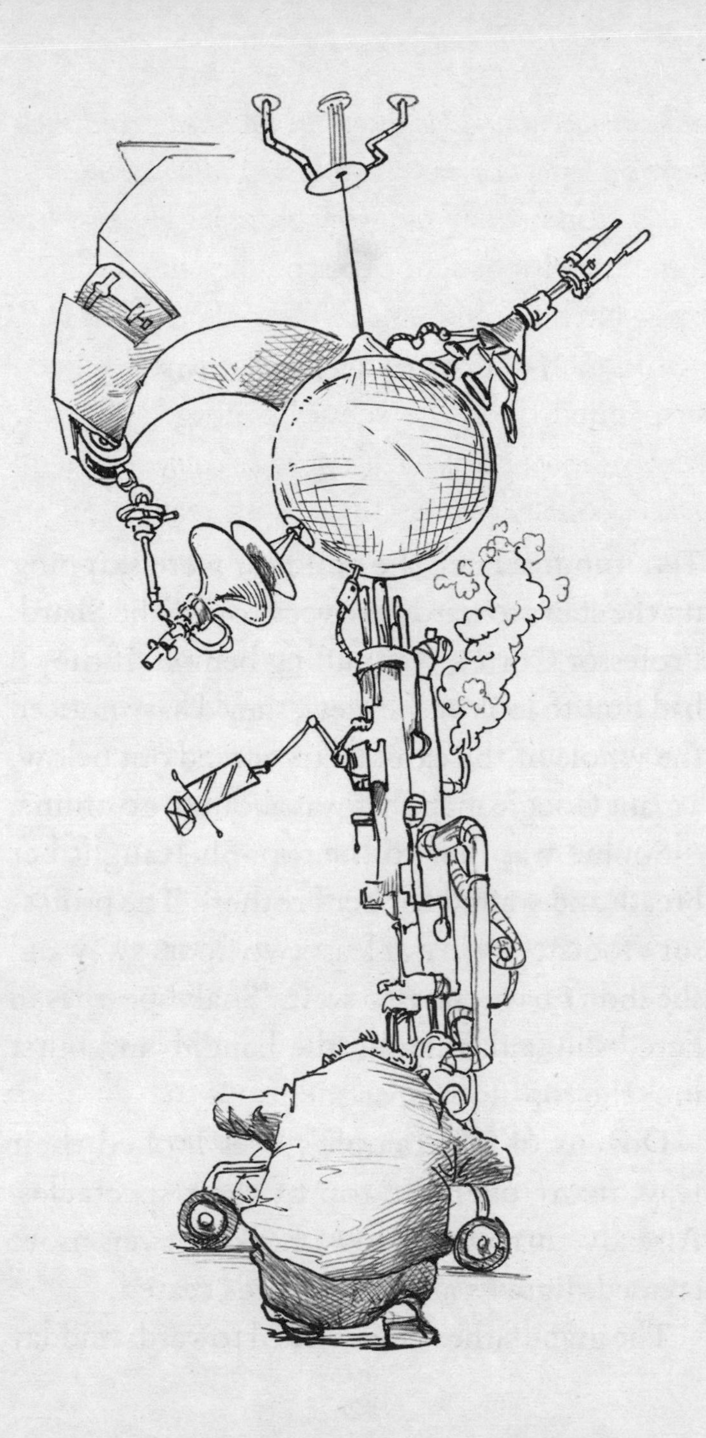

14. Getting Carried Away

Ten minutes later the children were skipping up the stairs towards the very top of the Shard. Professor Cortex was puffing behind. If they'd had time to look at the view, they'd have noticed the whole of the capital city spread out below, a giant Google map that was about to go offline.

Sophie was first to the top. She caught her breath and waited for her brothers. The professor's footsteps were at least two floors away and she didn't have time to wait. 'Shakespeare is in here,' she said, turning the handle, and burst into the top-floor apartment.

Dozens of old people's eyes looked their way, many over the top of their spectacles. Already furrowed brows became even more creased. Jigsaws and crosswords ceased.

The grandfather clock ticked towards midday

and the kettle boiled in an otherwise silent stand-off. The children stared at the small army of pensioners and the pensioners blinked back until the kettle boiled violently and clicked itself off.

'Young people,' said a voice, breaking the silence.

'I would imagine you'd like a biscuit?' suggested a helpful old lady.

Ben stepped forward first, his protective instinct taking over. 'We don't want your biscuits. We just want our cat back,' he demanded.

'And our diamond,' gasped the professor, stumbling into the room. 'The big one that was round the cat's neck. Long story, but it's not really ours . . .'

'Maximus,' smiled Maude. 'So good to see you again. But I'm afraid you're too late to save the world. Maybe you'd like a nice cup of tea instead?'

Shakespeare ran to Sophie and leapt up into her arms, the little girl squealing in delight.

'Where's the diamond?' demanded the professor. 'And can you please tell me why there are dozens of pensioners at the top of the Shard?'

'We're having a bit of a do,' said one of the old ladies. 'Aren't we, Gladys?'

'We're going back to the good old days,' agreed Edna. 'When I was your age,' she said, looking at the children, 'television was called books. The world today . . .' she began, before cutting herself off with a sigh, '. . . is ruined.'

'The world isn't ruined,' said Ben. 'It's just different.'

The man who was tending to a machine stood up and everyone fell silent.

He's clearly in charge, thought Shakespeare.

'We rather like the world as it was,' he said calmly. 'In the good old days. So I've invented a time machine that is going to take us back to the last millennium.'

'Good heavens,' spluttered Professor Cortex. 'You've worked out a way of distorting the space-time continuum? Did you have to reverse the polarities of the modulating flux capacitors or did you . . .'

'A *sort of* time machine,' interrupted the old man. 'But Maude's right. You are too late.' His bony fingers stretched towards a big red button. The room began to shake as the huge glass windows started to slide apart and the top floor

of the Shard opened up like a tulip on a summer's day. In less than a minute the sides had slipped away and the top floor had become an open-air apartment.

The wind whipped up and Edna lost her wig. Hundreds of jigsaw pieces scattered upwards and away into the London sky.

Barry had received the nod. He bent down and yanked at the lawnmower cord. The engine spluttered but failed to start. The Past Master looked frustrated. He nodded again and Barry yanked even harder; this time the engine spluttered into life and the Past Master fiddled with the machinery while it whirred into action.

Professor Cortex and the children had no idea what was going on. *This is my moment*, thought Shakespeare. *I have thirty-six seconds to save the western world from an Internet blackout*. The wind was howling and the old people were hanging on to their hats and dresses. Dorothy pulled her cardigan tighter.

The glitter ball had already begun to glow as Shakespeare launched himself from Sophie's arms. It wasn't so much a plan as an instinct. *I can't stop the machine*, he thought, but he remembered the Past Master saying that precision was everything. He knew that the satellites would be aligned in a few seconds, but that the slightest nudge would send the laser beams off track.

'Shakespeare!' yelled Sophie as she watched her cat take a running jump at the glitter ball. The little girl's hair swirled in the wind as he leapt higher than she thought possible. The glitter ball was glowing as Shakespeare hit it. He yowled in agony, the smell of singed fur blowing across the open-plan apartment, and his body landed in a heap. Ben held Sophie back as the ball grew brighter and a dozen beams of bright light shot harmlessly into the sky.

Shakespeare peered into the clouds, hoping he'd hit the ball with enough force to divert the lasers. He righted himself. His fur was smouldering, but he was very much alive. He ran to Sophie and curled himself round her ankles, the little girl crying with joy.

The Past Master looked up at the sky, horrified. 'You've ruined my plan,' he cursed, pointing a bony finger at Shakespeare. 'You've sent the lasers off course. You're an evil cat.'

Sophie hid Shakespeare in her coat. 'He's a hero,' she glared. 'He's put a stop to your wicked plan.'

They were very high up and the wind was howling. Cups and saucers whipped off the table into the city below. 'It's a bit blowy,' shouted one of the old ladies. 'Like the gale that brought the trees down in 1986.'

The Past Master knew that Plan A had been foiled so he went straight to Plan B: *Escape. Live to fight another day*. The old man walked calmly to his wheelchair. 'You've heard of the saying "it ain't rocket science". Well, this is!' he yelled, his voice trailing away in the wind. He pressed a button and wings flipped out of the side of the chair. Button number two ignited the engines, flames billowing out of the back. He fixed his goggles into place and struggled to strap himself in.

Shakespeare was proud of foiling the plan and thrilled at knocking the laser beams off target. *But the mission isn't over. There's no way I can let him get away*! The cat leapt out of Sophie's arms and launched himself at the wheelchair, gripping the man round the neck. *You're not allowed to escape, you evil baddie*. The old man tried to release the handbrake on his chair, but Shakespeare sank his claws in. The man gripped the feline scarf, trying to tear Shakespeare away from his neck.

Sophie, seeing her cat was in peril, threw herself at the wheelchair. The man screamed as the cat's claws sank in. He swatted Shakespeare and a ball of ginger hit the floor. Sophie landed on the launch button and the chair accelerated towards the edge of the eighty-seventh floor.

Dorothy spilt her tea as the jet-powered wheelchair was catapulted into the London sky.

Shakespeare righted himself, his head spinning. The wheelchair was spluttering into the early afternoon sky, the pensioner strapped in and Sophie's legs dangling off the edge. *That wasn't supposed to happen!*

Ben was yelling something that was lost in the wind. Shakespeare looked at the professor. He looked back, his face white and drawn, his mind whirring. You didn't need the biggest brain in the world to know that this wasn't good.

15. The Catsuit

'But it's untested,' yelled Professor Cortex as he pulled and stretched the Lycra suit on to the cat. 'I mean, it works in theory, but,' he gulped, 'we're a long way up and this isn't a theory.'

Shakespeare had conquered his fear of dogs. *And water's not as bad as it used to be. Now I've got the chance to tick 'heights' off too.*

All eyes were on the cat dressed in a tight-fitting orange suit. He stood tall like he'd seen superheroes do.

'The idea is that you hold your legs out and catch the wind,' yelled the professor. 'But, up here, it's very windy,' he said, stating the obvious. He carried the Lycra-clad cat towards the edge of the roof.

Shakespeare could see the microlite wheelchair wobbling in the near distance, Sophie's legs kicking as she struggled to stay aboard. He suspected it had been designed for one passenger and that Sophie's weight wasn't helping matters. If he'd thought things through, he wouldn't have done it. But he wasn't in thinking mode – he was in Spy Cat mode. *Rule number one! My favourite person in the whole world is in danger and I'm the only one who can help.*

'*Geronimooooo!*' wailed the cat, spreading his legs and plunging off the side of the Shard.

He remembered the professor saying that it's gliding, not flying. He recalled the video of the squirrels. They simply extended their legs and soared effortlessly through the air. 'Except it's not as easy as it looks,' he yowled, legs flailing as he whooshed past floors 86, 85, 84, 83 . . .

It was at floor 33 that he stopped scrambling and started gliding. His legs extended and instead of falling he started swooping.

'*Woaaa*,' he meowed, catching an upward current and zooming past the huge windows out towards the big city.

George and Jess were from America. They were dining in the Shard restaurant and George had been commenting that everything was

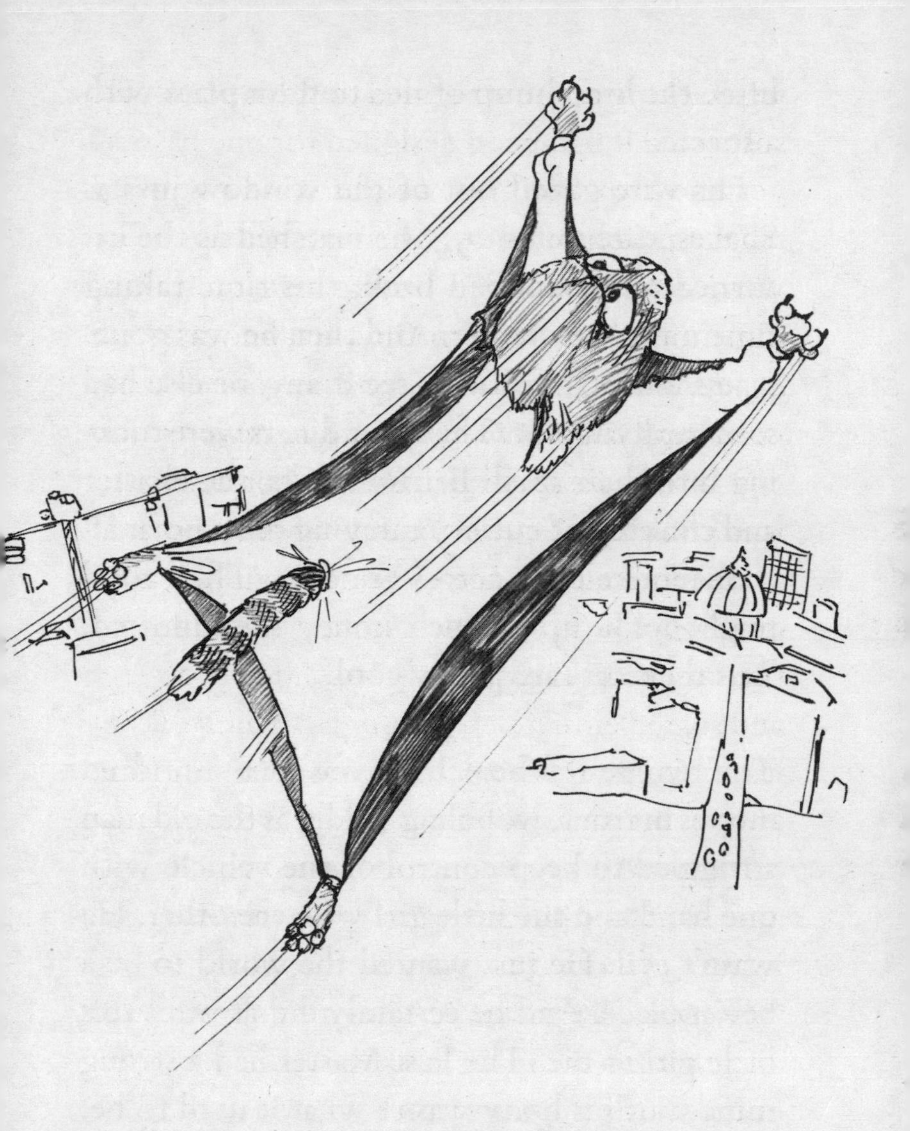

bigger and better in America. 'I mean, darlin',' he drawled, 'the Brits have Cheddar Gorge and we have the Grand Canyon. We have steaks the size of plates and the Brits have this . . .' He lifted the limp lump of meat off his plate with a fork.

His wife gazed out of the window just as Shakespeare sailed by. She watched as the cat turned and swooped back, this time taking time out to salute her. And then he was gone.

Jess looked around to see if anyone else had seen the flying cat. The other diners were tucking into their small British steaks, the chatter and clinking of cutlery carrying on as normal.

She looked out across London. 'Their food might not be up to much, honey' she admitted, 'but their cats are pretty cool.'

The winged wheelchair was one hundred metres in front, wobbling wildly as the old man struggled to keep control of the vehicle with one hand and the little girl with the other. He wasn't evil. He just wanted the world to be a better place. And he certainly didn't want this little girl to die. The Past Master had a strong mind, but his body wasn't what it used to be. The effort of hanging on to the child was taking its toll. Add in the excitement of flying across London and his heart rate was racing dangerously. 'Hang on,' he shouted. 'I'll try and land.'

The lawnmower-powered engine was already spluttering. There was a loud explosion and it stopped. Sophie had righted herself so she was sitting on the old man's knee, just like she had with her own granddad a thousand times. The balance was better, but the microlite wheelchair was now a glider instead of engine-driven. The only way was down. Sophie felt the man's grip loosen and she gripped the sides of the chair extra tight.

'Where are we going to land?' she yelled.

There was no answer. She wasn't sure whether he had died or just passed out. The only thing she knew was that she was going to have to land the craft herself.

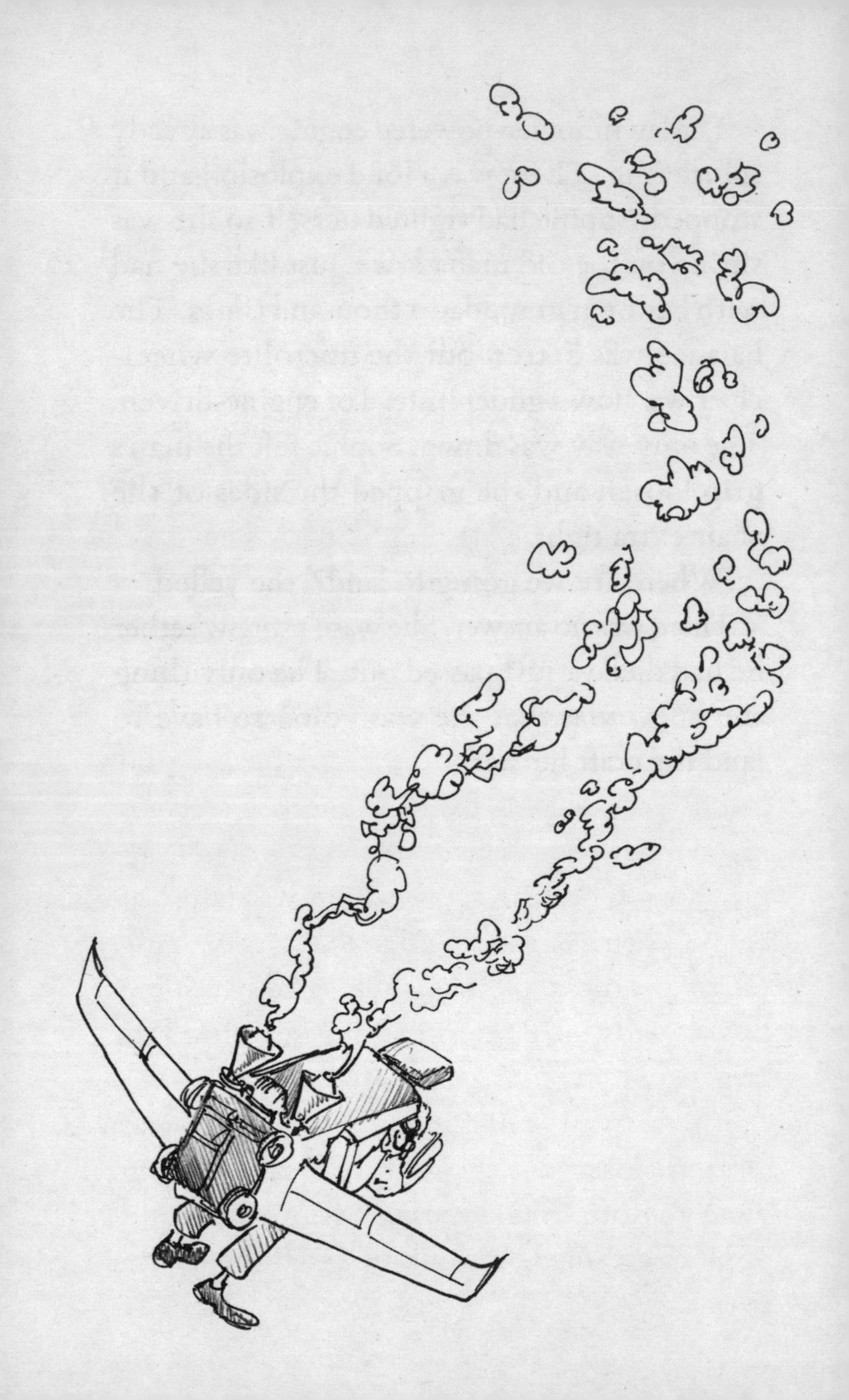

16. *Splash Landing*

Shakespeare was gaining. The wheelchair engine had stalled and the chair was falling a little too fast. Most cats weren't aware of Newton's law of gravity. They knew that if they fell out of a window they'd go downwards. And it annoyed them that birds could go upwards. Shakespeare's eyes were watering. Wind billowed into his cheeks, his face ballooning like a Cheshire cat. London was laid out below, the river snaking like the start of *EastEnders*. He tilted his body and started swooping downwards, a feline missile in search of its target.

Sophie was panicking. The ground was getting closer and the odds of a safe landing were remote. Shakespeare swooped by and Sophie screamed. 'I think he might be dead,' she yelled, her eyes bulging and her hair billowing. 'And I'm too young to die! *Help!*'

Flying squirrels are born with flaps of skin. That means, for them, it's normal to launch off trees and glide to the forest floor. Shakespeare had had exactly ninety seconds of practice as he swooped towards the wheelchair, attempting to dock. He recognized the London Eye below. And the Houses of Parliament. He was low enough to notice that London's roads were busy. *Typical London*, thought the cat. *Maybe the old man's right. Maybe there are too many people rushing around.*

Shakespeare zoomed past Sophie, yowling in frustration as he failed to make contact.

He lowered his left legs and turned for another go. Head down was fast. Head up was slower. He dive-bombed the chair, head down, pulling up at the last second, and landed, bat-like, clinging to the back of the chair, legs spread out behind him to cause enough drag to slow the wheelchair's fall.

Sophie looked delighted and terrified at the same time. 'Now what?' she yelled, her voice trailing away.

Shakespeare had a sinking feeling. He assessed

the situation and there was only one solution. He noticed people pointing upwards, cameras flashing as the makeshift glider plunged towards the capital city. *We're sure to get millions of hits on YouTube*, he thought. *Roads are full. People everywhere. There's only one solution. Water isn't my biggest fear. My biggest fear is losing the little girl I love the most in the entire world*. The River Thames sparkled below. *This calls for a splash landing!*

Sophie was squealing. The river was getting

closer and the winged wheelchair was descending too steeply. 'Tower Bridge is getting closer and we're nosediving straight for it. What are we going to doooo?' yelled the little girl. 'You can't swim! And what about the old man? He's strapped in. When this hits the water, it'll sink, taking him with it.'

Shakespeare felt calm. *The glider is going to hit the bridge. Guaranteed. If we're aboard when it hits the bridge, we'll all be dead. Guaranteed.*

The old man's eyes flickered open and his grip tightened round Sophie. 'I'm so sorry, little girl,' he said. 'This wasn't supposed to happen. We were just trying to slow the world down, so your generation could spend time playing outside.'

'What, learning to swim!' yelled Sophie, jabbing her finger at the grey Thames. 'It's a bit late for explanations. We need to get you out of this chair before we hit the . . .'

Shakespeare knew about the word 'sacrifice' and he felt calm. *Lives left? Nil.* It was a now-or-never moment. *Rule number one!*

Sophie's hands were raised in anticipation of hitting the bridge. He slammed a paw on the belt buckle and it sprang open. He stuck one claw into the old man's hand and one into Sophie's and extended to full range, raking them across their skin. *Sorry, folks!*

Both passengers screamed and let go, falling from the wheelchair and plummeting into the river.

Less than a second later the wheelchair slammed against the bridge. A thousand camera phones clicked, recording the crunching and scraping of metal. There was an agonizing screech as the chair slid down the wall and splashed into the water.

17. A Viral Hit

'One million hits in less than a week! That, Agent Pusskins, is quite an achievement.'

Shakespeare watched the video one more time, panic rising in his tummy. He watched the wobbly footage of the old man and his beloved little girl plunging into the water. Their heads bobbed up, Sophie cupping the old man's chin in her hand, her bronze lifesaving skills coming into use. The footage continued, focusing on the humans. Whoever had recorded the video had thought it best to commentate rather than jump in and help. 'Splash landing, dude,' said an American voice.

The camera phone quickly zoomed to the wreckage, the winged wheelchair sinking fast, and then back to the struggling swimmers. A boat had arrived and Sophie was being hauled aboard. 'Women and children first, man,' noted the commentator. 'And he must be her grand-pappy,' he continued as the old man's limp body was dragged from the water.

Shakespeare swallowed his panic, allowing pride to surface. *I'm not on camera*, he purred. He remembered the moment – the water swallowing him up. He'd heard of doggy paddle. *I guess this must be pussy paddle*, he thought. His legs were kicking hard. His mission had been accomplished. As he hit the water, he knew Sophie was going to be OK. *If I could survive, it would be a bonus.*

And, as a Spy Cat, I've learnt fast. His body had hit the water with some force. *I had the wind knocked out of me, for sure. But I wasn't going to give up*. He remembered Lara telling him a Spy Cat never gives up! *So I kicked harder than ever. But nobody saw a soggy cat. All the attention was on the people. The rescue boat made the water extra choppy*. Shakespeare gulped as he remembered going under again. *I thought it would be my final time.*

The Internet movie continued and his purring grew louder as he watched Sophie struggle to her feet and point at the water. She stood on the side of the boat, shouting frantically, jabbing her finger at the Thames. The commentator got excited. 'There might be another body,' he said hopefully. His lens scanned the grey water and he picked out a speck of ginger. 'OMG, man, it's a cat.'

It certainly is, thought Shakespeare, puffing his chest with pride and sitting tall for an ear stroke. *My little girl and me. We're a team*.

He watched as his frantic body was pulled out by a net and he was reunited with the squealing little girl.

Wet cat, wet girl, happy ending!

'Of course,' said Professor Cortex, tearing his gaze away from the computer screen, 'the science was actually quite simple. The Past Master, or "Eddie" as he now likes to be called, had worked on thermodynamics after the Second World War. He was way ahead of his time.'

'What are those thermal dynamics things?' asked Ollie.

'Thermodynamics,' repeated the professor, slowly and carefully. 'Diamond is a form of carbon,' he began, the science sparking him to life. 'Everybody knows that it oxidizes in air if heated to over seven hundred degrees Celsius.' He chuckled as if it was the most obvious fact in the world. He ploughed on, failing to notice the children's eyes glazing over. 'But what Eddie had rather cleverly noted is that, in the *absence* of oxygen, diamonds can be heated up to about three thousand degrees Celsius, which, let me tell you, is very hot indeed.'

I know, thought Shakespeare, licking a bald patch where his fur had singed away.

'This, you see, is at the limit of current scientific knowledge,' smiled the professor, peering at the children over the top of his spectacles. 'And that's where I like to be. Pushing the boundaries and all that.'

'Hang on, Prof,' snorted Ben. 'While the Past Master was experimenting on the edges of science, you were inventing a chocolate book.'

'Yes, well,' stammered the scientist. 'I'll admit that wasn't my finest hour. But the flying catsuit turned out all right, didn't it, Agent CAT? Anyway, Eddie had cottoned on to the fact that he could superheat the diamonds and use them to power a laser, or series of lasers . . .'

'That he would use to shoot down all the satellites that cover Europe . . .' continued Ben.

'Plunging us back into what he and his team call "the good old days". I've read his notes. Quite fascinating. They called it a "time machine". His plan was to go back to 1950 BC.'

'BC?' asked Ollie.

'Before Computers,' grinned the professor. 'When the world was simpler and the pace of change a little slower.'

'No Internet,' gasped Ollie. 'That'd be a disaster.'

'If his plan had worked, the world would certainly be a different place,' nodded the professor. 'Not necessarily any better or worse. Just different.'

Shakespeare had already pieced most of the adventure together, but two questions had been preying on his mind. He took a pencil in his mouth and approached the laptop. He clicked on Word and typed, 'why the shard?'

'Presumably,' nodded Professor Cortex, 'because it was already the highest place in Europe, he was closer to the sky.'

'Shard is xpensiv. He got money. Where from?' came the letters on the screen.

'That, Agent CAT, is a very good question. The police report indicates that, although his gang stole diamonds, they didn't ever sell any to fund their plan. Instead he had persuaded his followers, of which there were tens of thousands of old people, to donate their winter-fuel allowance to the cause. So he had millions at his disposal. He'd recruited followers from old folks' homes across the country. Some of them were desperate to go back to 1950 and giving up their winter-fuel payment was a small price to pay.'

'Just one more question,' said Ben. 'What's happened to Eddie and his team? I mean, they're not actually evil as such. They didn't want to hurt anyone. They actually thought their plan would be good for everyone.'

'It's a difficult one for the police,' agreed the professor. 'Stealing is most definitely a crime,' he said seriously. 'But, as you say, their reasons were fairly innocent.'

'What happened to the diamonds?' asked Sophie.

'They were returned to their rightful owners. Eddie made sure that hardly any of the old folks were actually involved in stealing diamonds, and the six of them that were have received what the courts call "community service". One hundred hours each. They've got to go into primary schools and talk to the children about "the good old days". You know, how life was different before computers and fast cars and ready meals.'

'Crikey,' said Sophie, 'that's like an actual *living* history lesson.'

The professor was beaming. 'And do you know what? The children are loving it. They're learning such a lot. And the old people are enjoying it too!'

'What about Eddie? He was the ringleader,' asked Ben. 'Is he in prison? I mean, he did some bad stuff. Didn't he?'

The professor looked around at the puzzled faces, each trying to work out if Eddie had actually done anything really terrible. 'He is doing a short stint in prison,' sighed the scientist. 'He planned all the diamond robberies and he really shouldn't have put Sophie's life in danger.'

The crowd nodded while the professor chewed the end of his spectacles. 'Although it's interesting that the police weren't sure what to charge him with. There's no law against inventing a flying wheelchair. The best they could do was charge him with criminal damage for shooting down the satellites, plus five diamond robberies and being in charge of a flying wheelchair without a pilot's licence.'

'I'm sure he'll be on his best behaviour and be out in a little while,' smiled Sophie. 'He held on to me ever so tightly.'

'Apparently he's working in the prison workshops, with the younger inmates, on a jet-powered mobility scooter. It seems that popping to the shops may soon be much quicker!'

'Coolio,' beamed Ollie, revving his hands like a motorbike. 'The wheelchairs could do wheelies. Maybe they could do a Fogeys' Formula One?'

'And,' noted the professor, 'we all owe a huge debt to the new cat on the block. If it wasn't for Agent CAT here, there would have been nobody to save the day.' He shuddered as he recalled Sophie shooting off into the London sky. 'Things could have turned out very badly indeed.'

'He's such a perfect puss,' said Sophie, squeezing her cat in her arms, her love spilling over into a silly scrunched-up face.

'You're a hero, Agent CAT,' agreed the professor. 'In fact, "Classified Animal *Trainee*" doesn't seem right any more. I mean, you are now a fully fledged qualified spy.'

Star and Spud wagged like mad. 'Welcome to the club,' yapped Spud.

'Proud to have you aboard, Agent CAT,' agreed Star. 'May you have many more successful missions.'

Shakespeare was busy thinking up a possible new name. *Classified Animal Spy. CAS? Or how about CAP? Classified Animal Puss. CAS is probably better. Or, if James Bond is 007, how about 00CAT?*

'So,' continued Professor Cortex, 'I've got a more appropriate name for you.'

Agent CAT held his breath, his collar and eyes blinking at the professor.

'I think we should call you . . . "Spy Cat".'

SPY PETS
SPY CAT
SUMMER SHOCKER!

Second-in-Command

Shakespeare woke with a start, his green eyes instantly wide and his claws extended. He scanned the room and his heart gradually stopped pounding. When you'd spent weeks living rough like Shakespeare had, you learnt to always be alert and ready to run – or fight. *After the last few weeks I've had*, thought the cat, *I'm lucky to be alive at all!* He looked around at Sophie's bedroom – pink curtains, cream walls and a pair of fluffy slippers. *Perfect*. Shakespeare stretched out luxuriously, hooking his claws into the super-soft bedding. *Peace and quiet and a nice comfy duvet, at last. What more could a feline want?*

The window was open and Shakespeare could hear some barking outside. His whiskers twitched nervously. *Bad memories*. He leapt effortlessly up on to the sill, being careful to stay hidden behind the curtain, and spied on the meeting below. *What a strange gathering of animals*. He looked at the black and white dog standing at the front of the group, clearly in charge. *She's the one who lives in this house*, Shakespeare realized. He always scampered away before she came back into the house, but he'd seen the children playing with her and petting her. He'd tried not to pay too much attention to the obvious love between them all. Shakespeare had no time for that sort of thing.

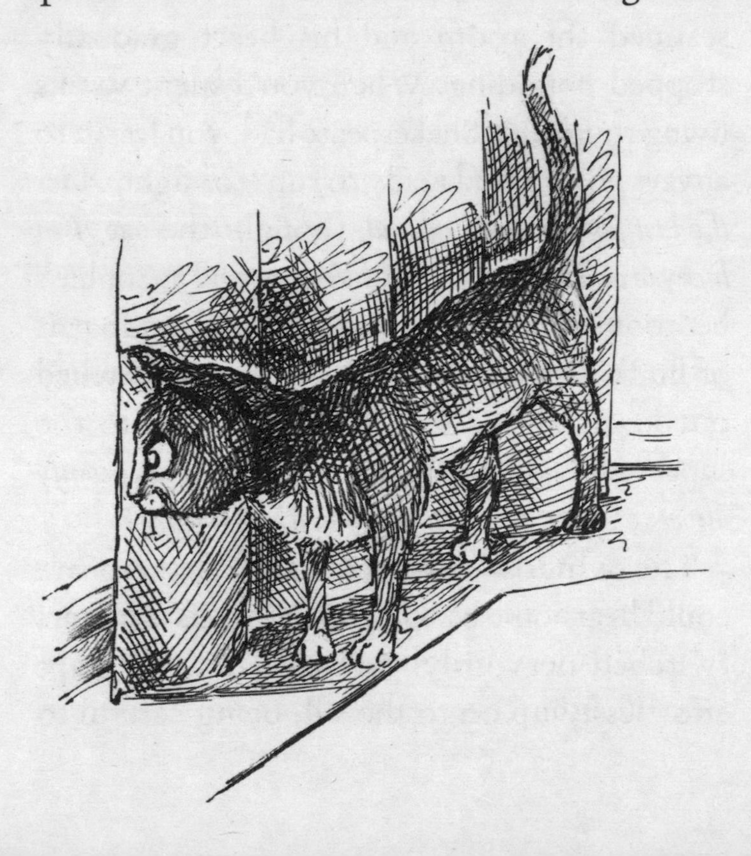

Her name was Lara. *Strange markings*, he thought. *And an even stranger ear arrangement*, he noticed as Lara's bullet-holed ear stood proudly to attention. Shakespeare listened intently. So she was a Spy Dog – whatever that meant. He wasn't even sure what a 'neighbourhood-watch team' actually was, but what appeared to be a competition to choose a leader to look after things while Lara was on holiday would be interesting to watch either way. It was always good to know who the competition was on your patch. He scanned the group below; there didn't seem to be anyone worth Shakespeare's attention. *But then*, thought the cat, *a life of action and adventure isn't really my thing*. Shakespeare was a loner. He only looked out for number one now. He cast an eye back to the warm bed that seemed to be calling him. *That's my thing!*

He listened to Lara's instructions, stretching a back leg and licking between his claws while he did so. 'The test is very simple. It's a feline versus canine challenge. We need to see who's cleverest, bravest and most energetic.'

Shakespeare continued listening and licking, his sandpapery tongue cleaning between his toes. 'Imagine there's a fire on the first floor of number 22. And there's a child asleep in the upstairs bedroom.'

'*Yikes!*' woofed the soppy-looking chocolate Lab. 'Best get there quick,' he said, bounding off towards the garden gate.

'Archie,' Lara bellowed. 'Heel, boy. I said *imagine*. Come back here and listen carefully to the instructions.'

Shakespeare sniggered. *Dogs are so stupid*.

'Yes, boss,' he woofed apologetically. 'But what about the fire?'

Lara sighed and shook her head. Shakespeare was surprised to see her eye the tortoiseshell cat with what looked like hope. *Interesting, not automatically rooting for her own species*.

'There's an *imaginary* baby at number 22,' Lara continued. 'And an *imaginary* fire. The first one to get into the house, upstairs, rescue the child and bring it back here is the winner, right?'

Archie looked chastened. 'Yes, boss.'

'I'm ready,' miaowed Connie, giving Archie a competitive sideways glance.

'Then what are you waiting for? Go!' woofed Lara as the cat and dog sprinted off in opposite directions.

Thirty seconds later Archie came panting back. 'Which is number 22?' he woofed.

Lara jabbed her paw after the cat, who was already halfway down the street. Archie bounded after her, a chocolate-brown bundle of enthusiasm.

Shakespeare watched lazily from above. He'd stopped licking but his back leg was still outstretched, in striking distance if the race got boring. The competition had become slightly less interesting now it was clear that the cat was going to wipe the floor with the daft dog.

Shakespeare had no time for dogs – *not stupid ones, not bossy ones like Lara, not vicious ones on the street and especially not the dog that got me evicted from my family.* It hurt him to think about it but sometimes he couldn't do anything else. Bad memories just popped into his head. The little girl had loved him so much. *A bit too much*, he considered. *So much that the dog got jealous. I just wanted a quiet family life but the mutt picked a huge fight, and when we were pulled apart I accidentally caught my owner with my claws and that was pretty much it.*

Shakespeare winced as he remembered being shouted at by the lady. *And the little girl was crying.* He'd then been palmed off on an elderly relative, far away from the little girl and his family. They probably meant well but meals were scarce and it just wasn't the same. Shakespeare had decided there and then that he would go it alone. He was going to survive all by himself. *So I left.*

He remembered catching sight of himself in a shop window two weeks later. *A stray!* he thought. *Imagine! Pampered puss to mangy moggy. Skinny ribs showing through my ginger fur. Homeless. Loveless. Living on the streets.*

Shakespeare shook his head, getting rid of the memories. He'd soon learnt to toughen up.

There were some angry dogs and very territorial cats in the neighbourhood to help him do just that. He looked in the bedroom mirror and admired his tummy, now puffed out with pride. His glossy fur – ginger except for three white feet – gleamed, and his green eyes and perky whiskers shone with health. *There's always an upside*, he considered, raising an eyebrow and giving a throaty yowl. *I'm a streetwise moggie*, he thought. *Grown up fast! I steal what I can, when I can. I don't need friends, or people, or a family. I'm a ginger ninja, it's me against the world.*

He was pleased with his current 'home'. *Three days and nights here*, he thought. *And nobody's rumbled me yet*. He'd decided to keep the family at arm's length. The little girl, Sophie, seemed friendly enough and had petted him in the garden, but so far so good. It was better that he didn't make attachments like before. Best to blend into the background. Hunt at night and find a nice snuggly duvet during the day.

Shakespeare looked back at the indentation in the duvet, imagining it might still be warm. *In a minute*, he promised. *The action below is just hotting up*.

It all started with a Scarecrow.

Puffin is seventy years old.

Sounds ancient, doesn't it? But Puffin has never been so lively. We're always on the lookout for the next big idea, which is how it began all those years ago.

Penguin Books was a big idea from the mind of a man called Allen Lane, who in 1935 invented the quality paperback and changed the world.

And from great Penguins, great Puffins grew, changing the face of children's books forever.

The first four Puffin Picture Books were hatched in 1940 and the first Puffin story book featured a man with broomstick arms called Worzel Gummidge. In 1967 Kaye Webb, Puffin Editor, started the Puffin Club, promising to **'make children into readers'**. She kept that promise and over 200,000 children became devoted Puffineers through their quarterly instalments of *Puffin Post*, which is now back for a new generation.

Many years from now, we hope you'll look back and remember Puffin with a smile. **No matter what your age or what you're into, there's a Puffin for everyone.** The possibilities are endless, but one thing is for sure: whether it's a picture book or a paperback, a sticker book or a hardback, **if it's got that little Puffin on it – it's bound to be good.**